ADVE

To Nicola Isele, Malika and Suzanne

LUBIN AND KLEYNER LTD.
114 West 119th Street
New York,NY 10026.
rrobinson72@hotmail.com

First published by Lubin and Kleyner 2002
10 9 8 7 6 5 4 3 2 1

A CIP catalogue record for this book is available from the British Library.

ISBN 0 9541570 0 1
Printed in Great Britain

ADVENTURES IN 3D

ROGER ROBINSON

Roger R

To Change
the direktor.

K

LUBIN AND KLEYNER LTD

CONTENTS

SIXTH DAN

If a woman wanted to break up with a man, she'd waste no time. She'd do it in an instant. She could be having the best time of her life only days before, but the morning she gets up and has the slightest niggling doubt, she'll say it's over, without remorse or even a second thought. A man on the other hand, if he wanted to break up with a woman he'd walk about for weeks, months, even years pretending to be happy. Men just aren't brave enough to face women and say it's over. They'd rather write a letter, say it on the phone, move hundreds of miles away – anything but face her like a man. They're just plain spineless.

In my case it had been two years since I'd first wanted it to end. Eventually I'd just had enough. I decided that I was leaving her once and for all. But the circumstances informing my fear of calling it off were not those of your average guy. My fear stemmed from the fact that she was a sixth dan of karate. For those of you don't know, there are only fifteen sixth dans of karate in the world. She was ranked in *Karate World* magazine as one of the top ten martial artists who ever lived. She kept a whole room just for golden trophies topped with small figurines frozen in punching and kicking positions. So, even though I'm six-foot-two and weigh in excess of two hundred pounds and she was a small-framed five-footer who weighed nine stone, I was afraid. I was afraid she'd beat me to a bloody pulp if she didn't take this break-up well.

The split would probably surprise her, because we'd been going out for six years, though in all that time I'd never been able to express my private thoughts to her. Every time I'd start to tell her a problem, she'd arch her eyebrows and furrow her forehead. That, combined with what seemed to me an evil glint in the hazel flecks of her eyes, gave me the distinct feeling of impending danger. After six years it'd pretty much become a habit that I don't complain, which probably led her to believe that everything was fine between us.

Believe me, you'd have kept quiet too, if you'd been to as many barbecues with her family as I have. The entire clan, every single one of them, are karate experts – from her mother and father, all the way down to her younger cousins. They'd spend hours telling long, detailed stories of all the great fights she'd won. Between mouthfuls of badly-cooked chicken, they'd say things like, "Remember that time when Kathy kicked that guy's lower jaw right out of his mouth? Hyuk, hyuk, hyuk!" They'd laugh till tears streamed from their eyes. Another would add, "Yeah, I remember that bottom row of teeth just hit the ground as if he spat them out! Hyuk, hyuk, hyuk!" One of them caught his breath to say excitedly, "Oh, oh! Remember the time when she cracked that guy's skull and he was just shivering on the floor like a big old jellyfish?" Then they'd all burst into another round of raucous laughter. Needless to say, I never had much of an appetite at those gatherings.

So, like I said, six years of those gory stories and you'd keep quiet too. But I didn't love her. I wasn't happy. It all built up to breaking point and I just couldn't take it anymore. I had to tell her, but I was terrified that she'd attack me and cause irreparable damage. I decided that I had to learn to defend myself.

I went to see my friend Brian about my predicament. Brian reckoned that he was an expert on martial arts, because he had a collection of over seven hundred and thirty kung-fu movies on video. He had scrutinised and analysed each film in ridiculous detail, from *Revenge of the Shaolin Monks* through to *Master Killer*. He had viewed and reviewed every chop, every block, every punch and every kick. He reckoned, in his selfmade-expert opinion, that the only style of martial arts that was undefeatable was the drunken master style. For those of you who don't know, the drunken master style consists of pretending to be drunk, preferably with bottles of alcohol in your hands, swaying around deliriously like you're unable to defend yourself and slurring your words as if you're completely smashed. The objective is to make your opponent think you're helplessly inebriated and mistakenly drop his guard, and then strike your enemy with a deadly force, using the very same bottles as weapons.

Brian gave me eighteen drunken master films on video. Every day, as soon as Kathy left for practice, I'd mimic every detail of the video, fighting imaginary foes in the living room. I studied every nuance and quirk. Day after day, I could feel myself getting stronger. Sweat would pour off my skin till I glowed as if greased. My abdominal muscles began to look more and more chiselled. As I punched the air, I could see the sinewy strands in my arm like plaited cable. For a month, I stumbled around the flat with a bottle of champagne in one hand and a glass of wine in the other, pretending to be drunk, studying every move in the videos, striking the air with the bottle at the right time but never spilling the drink in my other hand so I'd know that I was well-balanced.

Finally I was ready. I sat down to meditate upon my situation. Suddenly I thought I must be mad. I decided that my fears about her reaction were totally irrational. And there I'd been planning elaborate attack strategies! In the end, I convinced myself that I'd be alright, that I could just tell her and go book into some cheap hotel after all.

I decided I'd tell her that very evening.

At seven o'clock she came through the door. I told her there was something I needed to say. I sat her down on the couch and took a deep breath and rubbed my clammy hands together nervously. I blurted out that I wasn't in love with her anymore and that I had to leave because life with her had become unbearable. As I continued to stutter and stumble over explanation after explanation, I saw her eyes begin to sharply twinkle with that familiar evil look, but surprisingly, from one side of her curling mouth, she simply said, "If that's how you feel, then go."

I looked at her dumbfounded for a minute. I couldn't believe she would actually just let me go. I walked slowly out of the living room and ran up the stairs to the bedroom. I grabbed up the army duffel I'd packed in the morning, amazed to think that maybe I'd be able to come back for the rest of my stuff after all. I ran halfway down the stairs. She appeared at the bottom with her arms folded, staring at me with what I could only describe as a death glare. I slowed right down to a cautious walk. Still, she allowed me to walk by her into the narrow corridor leading to the outside door. I whispered an almost sweet "goodbye" as I reached for the door handle.

Then I heard the footsteps – running, gathering speed like a burning horse – in the corridor behind me. I turned around in time to see her flying through the air with a karate kick which landed with a thud in the centre of my chest. She shouted, "Over my dead body, you're leaving, you fuck!" I jolted backward and lost my balance and fell, banging my head against the copper doorknob. I nearly passed out but didn't, remembering all those days of training.

As she stood back in a cautious fighting pose to shame Bruce Lee, I crawled quickly into the kitchen and grabbed a bottle of port and another of champagne, taking large swigs from one bottle then the other, making wet, gulping sounds. Then I swayed around the kitchen, in a ridiculous parody of hopeless drunkeness, all the while waiting to pounce on her when the moment was right.

She looked at me closely. Her eyeballs bored into me as I staggered about the kitchen. I thought to myself excitedly, "It's working, it's working! She thinks I'm drunk! Boy, will I smash her face in with these bottles! Boy, will she be sorry she messed with me!"

The last thing I remember is her scornful voice. "Yeah, right, the drunken master style – this should be fun..."

ALIEN

I wake early and sit rocking back and forth with excitement. It should be here today. They promised it would be here today. The bell rings and I run out the bedroom door and down the stairs at a break-neck pace. The postman says, "Package for a – a – Roger Robinson."

I say excitedly, "Yes, yes, yes, that's me!"

"Can you sign here, please?" I grab the form and scribble my name on it somewhere and he gives me the package and I slam the door in his face and I turn around and run up the stairs to my room. I sit on the edge of the bed.

I can scarcely contain myself – I rip clumsily at the brown paper. Yes! I can't believe it's here! Oh, joy! My very own copy of *A Step-by-Step Guide to Making Crop Circles*. For so long, like everyone else, I'd been fooled into thinking that these elaborate field designs were made by aliens. I used to sit, astonished, looking at every documentary on television as, time and time again, they said that these were conclusive evidence that aliens were among us. Then I find this do-it-yourself crop circle guide at the back of a comic book for only £19.99 plus postage and packaging.

I start reading, frantically scanning each page for

what to do, how to do it and even sketches of suggested designs. I finish the book in just under three hours and run straight out the house to the hardware store to get all the stuff I need: some strong rope, some wooden stakes and a mallet – that's it! I'm so excited I can't stand still, but I somehow spend the day reading, sketching, planning, sketching some more. I wait until dark to take a train to the cornfields of Twickenham.

On the train I think about all the crop circles I'm going to make. It'll probably be on the news tomorrow. Scientists from all around the world will fly in to study my crop circles. I pull out the paper that I've sketched my first design on, being very careful that no one on the train can see it. The design is based on a book of constellations. That should be enough to get some scientists excited. My crop circles will go down in history as being the best and most elaborate crop circles ever.

I get to Twickenham and walk a mile to the nearest cornfield, with my knapsack full of wooden stakes, a mallet, some ropes and, of course, my sketches of the most elaborate crop-circle designs ever. I'm going to make crop circle history tonight, boy, you watch. I walk delicately between the corn stalks, making sure not to trample any stalks outside the intended circle itself and leave any clues as to how the circle was made. I choose the spot for the centre of my base circle carefully. I take out my first wooden stake and hammer it firmly into the soil, then loop a loose knot around it. With the rope extended to the desired diameter length, I begin to run in a circle, flattening all the stalks in the circle with the rope. As I run, I can feel the breeze like fresh mint on my face and the corn stalks grazing my body as I sprint round and round like a hundred-metre runner, grinning as I look back at the broken corn stalks behind me. As I complete the circle, I make one more lap for emphasis.

Finally, I walk to the centre of the circle and admire my handiwork with the beaming pride of the father of a newborn baby. I stop to pull out my design, looking for where to put the next circle in relation to the first. Having folded the map carefully and put it away in my knapsack, I bend down to wrench the wooden stake from the ground. Suddenly, a bright flash lights up the ground and for a second I think there's lightning on the horizon and my night of crop-circling might be rained off. But just as fast I realise that the bright light isn't a flash, but is dimming in a regular strobe pattern. I look up, slowly, and that's when I see it: a disc-shaped, chrome thing, about the size of a football field and it's hovering about fifty feet over my head. A number of small, glowing circles in its outer circumference change from fluorescent white, to yellow, to black and then back to white. I'm stunned. I cannot believe I'm having an actual extra-terrestrial contact, standing in the middle of a fake crop circle. This has got to be one hell of a coincidence, right?

Suddenly, I feel as if someone, something, is in the crop circle with me. Standing there, not fifteen feet away from me, at the edge of the circle is an alien, a real, live alien. He's about four feet tall, with this head at least two feet long. I read somewhere that aliens have to have huge heads, to accommodate their enormous brains. This one has two large, almond-shaped eyes that seem to spread round his face like a visor, with no visible whites to them, just completely black and with the sheen of plastic. His skin is smooth and grey, like a shark, and he has two small holes for a nose, and no mouth. His head tapers towards his chin, so his head takes on the shape of a guitar pick. His shoulders are narrower than his head, as is the rest of his body, and the fingers on his hands are half the length of his arms. You'd think I'd notice right off that he's holding a large sack with those fingers. Before I can move or speak, he's placed the sack on the ground and started rummaging through it. He quickly pulls out half a dozen wooden stakes, a mallet, some rope and a piece of paper.

He walks towards me in tiny steps and hands me the paper. I can't believe it – it's a design for a crop circle! But this design is far more advanced than anything I could ever imagine. He points to me and then points to the map and then points to himself. I'm standing there with my mouth hanging open, and it dawns on me: he's offering me an opportunity to make crop circles with a true master. I nod my head as enthusiastically as the situation will allow. He turns and walks to the edge of the circle, beckoning me to follow with a curving movement of one of his long fingers. I follow tentatively, a dozen paces behind, as he disappears between the corn stalks.

We stop about fifty feet away from the first circle and, pointing to a spot on the ground, he hands me a mallet. I start hammering one of the wooden stakes into the ground. We both loop ropes around the stake and pull them a full hundred metres in opposite directions. The alien dips his head as a signal and we start running. Even though his legs are very short and I'm no slouch, he overtakes me several times, leaping over my rope with a weird little hop as he passes me in the opposite direction. By the time I've made one complete circumference, he's already made three. The effect of our dual efforts, combined with his amazing speed, is that the corn stalks aren't just pressed down flat, they're practically ground down to cornmeal.

When we finish, we step into the centre of the circle to survey our work. The edges of the circle are so precise, so perfect, I nearly break down, trembling with pride. I know that I'm apprenticed to a true artisan. There's no time to dwell on the finer points – already he's walking through the corn stalks, reading his map, looking for the next location.

All night, until nearly dawn, we make circle after circle, each one more beautiful and complex than the last, with the most incredible configurations. By five o'clock, I know we're both getting tired because when he's running one of his laps, instead of jumping over my rope he trips on it, pitches up in the air with a somersault and falls about five feet away. I think, Oh, my God, I've killed him! The first alien friend I've ever made and I've killed him! Just when the night was going so well, too. I run up to him. By the time I get to him, he's lying really still, just staring up at the sky.

Suddenly, as if he's just regained whatever consciousness aliens regain, he shakes his head and stands up. For a long minute, he's just looking at me like he's never seen me before. Then he starts holding his stomach and bending over, rocking up and down. At first I think he's in pain, but then it dawned on me that he's laughing! I can't help it, I start to laugh, too. I laugh until tears roll down my cheeks, until my stomach hurts, until I fall over with my knees bent and my hands clutching my belly. He points at me and laughs even harder, but with no sound, just bending over more and rocking harder and slapping his knee periodically. Of course, this makes me laugh even more. Tired from a night of circles and laughter, we lie side by side like school friends, looking up at the stars.

I ask if he wants to come to my house for breakfast, to see if our crop circles make it onto the morning news. He nods his head in agreement. Somehow he signals to his ship, which is still hovering in the distance and it disappears in a flash.

Cool as it may be to have an alien for your new best friend, the problem I'm looking at is how to smuggle him onto the train to my house without anyone noticing he's not exactly human. I give him my hooded coat and pull it over his head. He's so short that the jacket hangs down to his ankles and I convince myself he looks like he could be my kid brother. We walk slowly to the train station, trying to act natural, whatever natural is when you're strolling through pre-dawn suburban streets with an alien in a puffa jacket. We get to the station and find the trains to London don't start running until 5:45 – another twenty minutes.

We sit in the warmth of the waiting room and every so often he tries to pull the hoodie back and I have to yank it quickly back over his enormous head – we're alone, but anyone could walk in at any moment. Naturally, it's not long before someone does, an old lady on her way to her cleaning job, judging by her clothes. She sits directly opposite us, staring at the both of us while we try to burn holes in the floor with our eyes, our heads down and very still. I can feel her staring and staring and staring at us. I'm thinking CNN, I'm thinking CIA, I'm thinking why the hell doesn't she have any knitting? I'm thinking we're caught for sure. Out of nowhere, she says, "He's a bit young to be up this early in the morning, isn't he?"

"Pardon?' I say.

"I said, it's a bit early to have a youngster up, isn't it?"

"Oh – oh – uum – he doesn't get up this early everyday – it's a special day – going to London to see his grand–"

At this moment, the damned alien suddenly tries to pull down his hood again, but I pull it back over his face, patting his back hard enough to nearly knock him out of his seat and squeezing his shoulders with what I hope will be taken for affection.

The old woman starts rummaging around in her huge bag and pulls out a packet of chocolate biscuits. She offers the packet to the alien, and he reaches out to take one! And here I am thinking aliens are smarter than humans. I grab it from her before he gets his hand out of the sleeve, though I can't help wondering why he bothers, considering he doesn't have a mouth and couldn't eat it anyway. "It's a bit too early for chocolate biscuits, I think," I say.

"Oh, I'm sorry." She seems a little surprised to see me snatch the biscuit like that.

"It's alright, I'll have it," I say and I jam it whole into my mouth and chew, even though I hate chocolate biscuits.

After another hundred years, the train arrives and we walk to the very end until we find an empty carriage. Every commuter who gets on the train between Twickenham and my stop seems unusually interested in us, but since none of them actually looks in our direction, I reckon I'm just a little nervous.

We make it off the train and up the street to my house before it's even properly light, and no one raises any alarms. I open my door and wave the alien in first. He negotiates the stairs with his short steps and I guide him into the living room, where he sits on the couch with his feet dangling six inches above the floor. I turn on the TV and he sits watching the basketball play-offs live via satellite from California, while I go into the kitchen to make some bacon and eggs and a fried slice. Making crop circles all night sure works up an appetite. I come back with the food just in time to see the beginning of the news. "In the main headlines this morning, a fresh series of crop circle formations is baffling farmers and scientists alike. Is this conclusive evidence that UFOs exist? Join us after the break when we hear from three leading scientists with several different theories but one area of agreement: these circles cannot be explained for certain."

I look at the alien, with the world's biggest grin and say, "We've done it!" He raises his hand and gives me a high five, just like the basketball players he's been watching, and then clutches his stomach and begins to laugh again. We laugh until the news programme's over. For the first time in my life, I'm so excited I can't even eat my breakfast.

GLOW

So here I am in the club, with my arms around Charmaine. Charmaine had been the object of my childhood adoration, a crush which had gained strength daily as we grew into adulthood. The rest of the guys are sipping cocktails and giving me the thumbs up every time I glance in their direction. I know every single one of them is wishing that he could be where I am right now. You see, in Ilford nothing much ever happens. Well, if it does, it happens to someone else.

Back when we were kids, Charmaine moved to America with her parents. Ten years later, she comes back for a summer holiday and of course her status has gone from pre-teen town beauty to triumphant travelled queen/goddess.

That's why I feel so good about our bodies pressed tightly against each other while a slow tune serenades us in the club. With every dance we press harder and harder into each other and we even keep right on holding each other through the fast tunes until the slow tunes come around again. I feel wrapped in a passionate locked link, while the club around me dissolves into this one moment.

Then my stomach starts convulsing with the most painful cramps I've ever had. Convinced they've been brought on by all the nervous excitement, I make an excuse to Charmaine. In the toilet, I look at myself in the mirror, staring into my own eyes, trying to will myself to regain my composure. The cramps finally settle and I begin to walk back to Charmaine and the guys.

As I walk out of the toilet, I see people staring at the front of my trousers, whether astonished or amused I can't tell. Instinctively, I reach down, thinking that my trousers must still be unzipped, but the zip is shut tight. So I look down.

There it is, in quiet repose, glowing like a small green plutonium rod or a very small Star Wars light sabre. It's glowing right through the Levi's dark denim jeans I'm wearing. I stare at it for a few seconds, completely flabbergasted. Then I look up at everybody crowded around, staring at it. It slowly dawns on me that they can see its exact size, its exact shape. A few of them manage to look me in the eye, as if to say, What the fuck is that? And why is it glowing? I have no idea.

My next thought comes much quicker. "Oh, my God! What if Charmaine sees it in its resting state and thinks it's really small? Worse yet, what if she sees it and thinks that any glowing green dick is just plain nasty, no matter how big it is?"

I push past the drunken crowd, hoping they'll think they imagined it, and take off my leather jacket to tie around my waist. I just about manage to say goodbye to Charmaine, promising I'll call her, and make a hasty exit from the club without even thinking about the guys I've come to the club with.

As you'd expect, I drive home wondering what the hell is happening to me. At every red traffic light, I lift up the leather jacket to see if it's still glowing. It is. Every time, just before I check, I can't help hoping it's back to normal but, no, there it is, glowing merrily and giving off a green tint which lights up the inside of the car. Passing drivers seem to slow down – they must be able to see the glow. All I need now is a curious cop to pull me over.

I get home and turn on the lights and just as quick I turn them back off again. For ten minutes straight I sit there, hoping that somehow the glow will turn itself off, too, eventually.

Frustrated and confused, I go to bed, transfixed by the glowing green beacon in the middle of my sheets. I don't sleep much. I wake up the next morning to a ringing phone. It's Jake asking me what the hell happened and how come I just ran out on Charmaine like that when things were looking so good. I lie and tell him that I'd suddenly gotten really sick, which isn't exactly a lie unless you consider a fluorescent green penis a sign of good health. He tells me that after I left she came across to Jake and the guys almost in tears, asking them why I left so suddenly. She asked them if I already had a girlfriend, said that really the only reason she'd come back from the States was to see me.

"Do you still like her?"

"Of course I do, man. I just got sick, OK?"

"Then you'd better call her, because every single guy I know is gearing up to make a move on her after last night. Give her a call right now, mate, right now."

Feeling more stressed than I've ever felt in my life, I pick up the phone, wanting to undo the damage. Then I ask myself, what the fuck am I doing? What can I possibly tell her? "Sure, baby, come on over to my flat for a candlelit dinner – I've got my own private candle all lit up just for you?" I just set the phone gently back in its receiver. Fuck.

Two days pass and I'm still fluorescent. I don't leave the house and I don't call her, or anybody else for that matter. The phone rings while I'm in the toilet, trying to decide if it's glowing a little less today. I come out to hear Charmaine's exasperated voice. "I thought you were going to call me? Have I done something to upset you? Please give me a call. I just want to talk." I listen in anguish. No way can I pick up the phone, though there is absolutely nothing else I want more in the world just then. I just can't imagine what I'd say. How I'd explain.

The phone rings again and I let the answer machine get it. It's Jake. "Hi, Dwayne. Me and the guys are coming over to check up on you and –"

I pick up the phone. "Hi, Jake."

"Oh, so you're there. What, you're screening your calls now?"

"No, I was just in the toilet, OK?" I know I sound defensive.

"Are you alright, man? You've been acting pretty weird the past couple of days. Why haven't you been out of your house? And why didn't you call Charmaine, for God's sake?"

"Uh, I've got a lot on my mind right now."

"No one has that much on their mind! Anyway, me and the guys are coming over to check up on you."

Before I can even blurt out a word of discouragement, he's hung up the phone. I'm panicking fast. I don't know what to do. I know no way can I let the guys see my dick glowing like some fucking alien. But just then I have an idea. Nobody saw my privates glowing at the club as soon as I wrapped my leather jacket around my waist. And maybe no one would realise that my dick is fluorescent green if I wore trousers of exactly the same colour.

I'm on the phone to the Ann Summers sex shop in Soho faster than a robot can speed dial. "Do you have leather underwear?" No preamble, no polite chat – I'm desperate.

"Yes, we do, sir."

"OK, and do you stock fluorescent green pants?"

"Yes, but only in fifty percent lycra stretch-to-fit style."

"Can you deliver today?" My heart's going wild.

"Sure, but it'll cost extra if we use a courier."

"Great! Anything!" She must think I'm nuts.

So I read out the digits on my Amex card and pay ridiculous money for delivery within four hours. It's worth it, I figure.

I sit around the rest of the afternoon, praying that the package will be delivered before the guys arrive. I call the shop on the hour to ask if it's gone out yet, where the courier is en route and how much longer it'll take. Finally, finally, the bell rings. A moment of panic while I try to divine whether it's the sex shop courier on the other side of the door, or the guys.

I open the door.

"Leather underwear, small, and lycra pants, fluorescent green, for one Dwayne Powell. Sign here. Here's a free brochure for new customers."

I grab the package and slam the door. Right there, I fling off my tied-around leather jacket – I didn't even want complete strangers to see me glowing, even if they do work in a sex shop where not much can come as a surprise. I pull on the green pants and it works. I could barely even see the glow. The only problem is that they're so tight you can see everything else, if not the glow.

The bell rings again and this time it's the guys. I open the door quicker than they expect. Clutching pizza and beer, they stare me up and down, from my grey flannel hoodie to my figure-hugging florescent green pants, all the way to my Nike Air Jordans. They stare long and silently. I tell them to come in.

They sit and pop a few beers and make nervous small talk between themselves. Then Jake comes right out with it. "I can't take this anymore. Dwayne, me and the guys have something to ask you. Are you gay?"

I nearly choke on a mouthful of pizza and ask,

"What the hell would make you think that?"

"Well, first you bluntly refuse to sleep with Charmaine, and secondly, uh, your new, more extreme fashion sense," looking down at my tight green pants, "and the Ann Summers brochure on the TV and the unopened package of leather underwear on the floor..."

I sit there with my mouth open, seeing his point completely but having no idea what to say, and all the guys are frozen, staring, waiting for some answer.

Finally Jake says, "Well, are you? Are you gay? Because if you are, it'll still be cool with us. We'll still be your friends."

"Jake, I'm not gay."

They let out a collective sigh of relief. Jake says, "Then what's going on with you, man?"

"Look, I know it looks weird but I can't explain right now what's going on, but I promise I'll explain it to you later. Soon." Then I tell all of them that they have to go.

"Can we at least finish our beers and the pizza?"

"No. Everybody's got to go now. I don't feel well..."

As I usher them out, their faces seem more confused than when they came. I close the door and throw myself on the bed in complete frustration. Before I can even thump the pillow, the door buzzes again.

"Who is it?"

"It's Charmaine."

I say nothing.

"If you don't let me in right now, I'm going to book

myself on the first flight back to New York and you'll never see me again."

I can't let her leave, I just can't. I open the door and she walks in tentatively, sits on the couch, waiting for me to say something. I sit next to her and she floors me by taking my hand and bursting into tears.

"What's going on between you and me, Dwayne? I mean, I come all this way to see you and you won't even give me a simple phone call, let alone a date? I just saw the guys down the road and they said I shouldn't waste my time because you're gay. Is that true, Dwayne? Is it?"

"No, baby, that's not true. Those guys don't know nothing."

"Then prove it to me," she says, as she leans forward and kisses me. Overcome by years of fantasy and longing, I kiss her passionately. She peels off my grey flannel hoodie and slides out of her tiny top. Her breasts hypnotise me, and while I'm lost in kissing them, she tries to pull down my pants.

I say, breathing hard, "Wait! Before you do that, I have something to tell you. And then you might not want to."

She presses her fingers to my lips and says, "You wait, Dwayne. I have something to show you first."

She takes two steps back and as the world slows almost to a stop, she begins to unbutton the top of her lady-cut Levi's. Fluorescent green rays shoot from her crotch like laser beams and she just smiles and smiles and smiles.

NIGHTSTICK

I can't believe what I have to go through for some basic comforts. Nothing extravagant, just some basic comforts-like a roof over my head. I glance at the petrol gauge and the needle lies between empty and not quite empty. The last thing I need right now is to stall. I search my pockets for some money. Finding none there I open the glove compartment and search over and around the expired insurance and MOT. I find a scattering of change. Sixty-two, sixty-three, sixty-four, sixty-five pence, there is just about enough to get some fumes. I pull in at the first station.

I insert the gas nozzle and squeeze the handle ever so gingerly. Sixty-three, sixty-four... sixty-eight – SHIT! I open the car door and search the floor and the seats for the extra three pence needed. I'm already running late. I walk up to pay at the window. I casually drop the collection of loose change and try to walk away, the cashier shouts and taps on the protective window and like a fool I turn back.

"Three pence short." While signalling with three fingers on his left hand.

I feign an expression of complete surprise and pretend to search my pockets, then I say, "Look, I'm sorry, I don't have any more money."

"Then why is it you take gas if you don't have any money?" he asks in strong jerks of his Asian accent.

"It's only three pence for God's sake. I can't believe that you're making a big issue of this."

"Only three pence! Only three pence you say! If I say only three pence to thousand customers today, that would be three hundred pounds from my pocket. I lose my house and my children don't eat and I be begging on street, bringing shame to my family. And further more, taking and not paying is stealing and if you don't pay I call police." Illustrating his intent by holding up the receiver to his ear.

I stand there with a pained expression, thinking to myself, why for once in my life can't something fall effortlessly in my favour? Why is it that I have to battle with everything and everybody?

The last thing I need tonight is the police after me. So I start looking on the ground and there I see a gleaming twenty pence piece pressed into the asphalt. I stoop down and dig it up with my car keys. I step back to the counter and slam down the twenty pence and shout, "Here's your damn three pence. I hope it feeds your family and saves you from homelessness."

I get in the car and slam the door and screech my tyres in disgust. I feel like there's a knot at the back of my neck. The intermittent glare of the lights in the rear-view mirror is beginning to hypnotise me. How in God's name did I get to this? I mean I don't even smoke and here I am cruising down the highway with two kilos of compressed weed in the back of my car. How did I get to this?

Well my first mistake was to think that that measly part-time job could afford me a flat of my own, but I just had enough of living with my mother. I mean, I was a grown twenty six-year-old man living in my mum's house and the Church is her life. Not that I had anything against Jesus, God or the Church. I mean even I would go to the obligatory Christmas, Easter and New Year services. The problem was that my mother thought that everyone should obey the Bible literally. I couldn't take it anymore. I couldn't even bring a woman home to spend the night without my mum bursting in the room with a Bible giving a full-on sermon about Satan and fornication. Every time I made love I'd have to put a pillow over my girlfriend's face to muffle the sound. So I had to leave there if I wanted to have any kind of sex life. So I finally got together enough money to get a flat and decided that the time had come to make that move. That day was the worst, my mother was mumbling all these comments under her breath about fleeing from a house of God into the arms of Sodom and Gomorrah, and I was shouting to her that God does not want fanatics in his religion. She shouted back, once I go over to the side of the Devil not to come back to her house. I yelled that I wouldn't go back to her house even if it were the last house left standing in a hurricane. It was all very dramatic.

So I finally had my own place. I must admit it wasn't the most beautiful, but it was cheap and it was mine. I thought I could save up enough money and buy some furniture in a few months, perhaps finish decorating in a year or two. My own flat. I thought it would be great having my girlfriend over anytime I wanted without hiding.

My girlfriend started coming over, but after a while she started complaining. Complaining about eating microwave dinners with plastic knives and forks, complaining that the mattress hurt her back. She kept nagging and nagging and dropping subtle hints about she needs a man who could provide for himself and that she isn't accustomed to this kind of living and that Michael this lawyer guy invited her for a business weekend in New York.

So this got me thinking, perhaps she's right, perhaps I wasn't the most motivated brother in the world. Maybe I did need to take a hold of my life. So against my better judgement I went to my supervisor and told him I needed more hours and I deserved a raise. This bought a semi smile to his face, which made me feel good at first. Then the semi smile burst into fully-fledged raucous laughter, which became mocking and then developed into an outright insulting cackle. He caught his breath and said to tell it to the owner of the supermarket. He said that I should pop in his office right now that he was waiting to see me.

I walked up the stairs to his office all puffed up with the spirit of get ahead. Then it happened.

Mr Jones said, "Before you sit down, I'm afraid I have some bad news for you. We have to let you go."

"What? Let me go? You mean, like, let me go to another branch?"

"No, you're sacked."

I began to beg, "Please, please don't sack me, please. I'm begging you, please."

I began to see visions of me losing my flat and my girlfriend. I started to cry right there in the owner's office. I fell to my knees, I rolled on to my back, my hand outstretched to his now upside down image. My tears flowed up the side of my forehead, crying out, "Ple e e e e eease don't do this, please? I'm begging you, begging!"

He then proceeded to call security. No matter how I tried I couldn't keep myself from sobbing hysterically as these gorilla security guards were carrying me as easily as an empty cardboard box.

They deposited me right outside the store in a crumpled heap, numb with grief. I must have sat there for over two hours. I didn't even notice when they closed up. My only thought was what I was going to do. I had left my mum's house with such a flourish that I had way too much pride to go back there, and I thought my girlfriend would definitely leave.

I got up, the hard cement made my bottom sore. I walked towards the car and drove home. I opened the door to my damp flat and lay down on the mattress. I pulled the covers over my head and tried to go to sleep. I heard the phone ring but I let the answer machine get it because I wasn't in the mood to talk to anybody. I just wanted to sleep.

I eventually got up later that evening and checked the message. It was John saying he had heard what had happened. I thought, fucking great, now everyone knew, but then he said to call him back because he might be able to help out my situation. I wondered how John could help me when, back in the day, I used to have to lend him money.

So he told me how much money he had made transporting weed from suppliers to sellers. All he did was put a few kilos of weed in his car and drive it where it had to go. He said sometimes he'd make four or five drops a night and that there was too much business and because I used to help him out he was prepared to pass some business my way. I knew I'd do it as soon as I realised that one drop would pay for my flat for two months, help me get some furniture, help me keep my girlfriend and give me some space to find a job.

So now I'm here on this highway. I just want to get there, collect my money and move on with my life. I'm so stressed that I'm sucking on a spliff and I don't even smoke. Hell, they wouldn't miss one spliff from the two kilos in the trunk. You know what, I'll take my girlfriend to New York for the weekend and I'll buy myself some sneakers. I sure hope nothing funny happens at the drop off.

I should have got a gun for some protection. What am I thinking? Even if I had a gun I'd be too nervous to use it. Oh no, I've just had a thought: what if they have guns and shoot me and steal all the weed? Or even worse if they just wound me and steal the weed and the sellers think I stole their money and put a contract out on my head? Calm down, Roger, this weed is getting you paranoid. Everything will be fine.

What's that flashing light? Please be an ambulance. Oh shit, it's a police car. Shit, shit, shit, shit! Half of me is saying, keep cool, the other half of me is saying, run or else you'll spend the next thirteen years in jail.

Oh no, he's telling me to pull-over. I pull-over, take two deep breaths and try to relax myself. He pulls his car behind mine. I can see him in the rear-view mirror saying something into his radio, all the time keeping a keen eye on the car. His stoic face gives no clue to his mood. He comes out of the car slowly, ambling towards my car with his hand firmly placed on his nightstick. I feel like a man at the gallows who knows at any minute the floor could give way beneath him.

I repeat a mantra of, "keepcoolkeepcoolkeepcool". As he draws closer I can see his torso in the rear-view mirror. The silhouette of his black uniform becomes more clearly visible with every blue flashing light as he advances. Think, Roger, think. This ain't no joke. This is the rest if your life right here, right now, and this is it.

"Good evening, officer. What seems to be the problem?"

"Are you aware that your left indicator light isn't working? Can I see your licence, insurance and MOT, please?" I hand them to him and he peruses the documents for a few seconds. "Do you know that your insurance and MOT have run out, Mr, uh, Robinson?"

"Oh, really? I didn't realise."

"Where have you just come from?"

" My friend's house."

"Where is that?"

"In Hackney."

"What were you doing there at this time of night?"

"Talking."

"Have you been drinking at all?"

"No."

"Can you tell me why your eyes are so bloodshot Mr Robinson?" Raising his eyebrow with the first hint of suspicion that showed on his face.

"OK, OK, officer. I'll tell you the truth. To be honest I've been smoking this little spliff. It's all I have and if you want to take me down to the station for this tiny spliff then it's up to you. To be honest I don't really smoke, but I've been having a bit of trouble with my girlfriend and I was feeling a bit wound up so I had a little bit to relax me a little, you know what I mean?

He stares at me for a few seconds his eyebrows still raised and says, "Stay in your car, please!"

He walks back towards his car with decidedly more pace than he left it and talks on the radio for a couple of minutes that seem to pass second by second. He walks slowly back and asks, "Have you ever been arrested Mr Robinson?"

"No."

"Do you have anything in the trunk of your car?"

"No."

"Step out of the car and open the trunk, please, Mr Robinson." I grip the steering wheel and freeze. My eyes flitter from side to side and I wonder what to do. "Mr Robinson, please step out of the car – NOW!"

He unclips his nightstick and draws it out from his holster. I can see it in the corner of my eye. I look straight ahead, rigid with fear, wondering how to get out of this. He takes the round tip of the nightstick and presses it at the side of my neck. I think to myself, there's no way I'm going to jail for this. I have to make my move now.

"Mr Robinson don't make problems for yourself!"

He presses the nightstick harder into the side of my neck. I have to make a move now or else it will be all over. I turn my head slowly and start lightly kissing the nightstick's dark round tip with light tiny kisses. The policeman's eyebrows raise in unison, then his expression melts into pleasure as his eyes start to roll back into his eyelids and I begin to suck hard with my lips on the tip of his nightstick, before taking it fully into my mouth. The shiny saliva on the stick contrasts with the matt black part that has not yet entered my mouth. He starts groaning in the rhythm of the stick entering and re-entering my mouth. He leans over the top of the car and starts banging on it with the fist of his free hand. I can see he is nearly there so I try to wrap it up. I start, trying to swallow up as much as I can, just stopping short of choking on every inward thrust and sucking as hard as I can as it is pulling out, as if I don't want it to leave my lips, the stroke of the nightstick as constant as a piston on a steam engine picking up speed. All the time I'm sucking the nightstick I'm thinking I can't believe the kind of things I have to go through for a normal life. Nothing fancy, just some basic comforts-like a roof over my head.

The policeman's increased grunts bring me back to the situation. He starts to moan. Oh, ohh God, oh God! His body stiffens, begins to shudder, and then his body relaxes into a slump over the roof of the car.

After about a minute of heavy panting, he stands up straight, trying his best to avoid looking in my eyes. He straightens his hat and uniform as best he can and clips his nightstick back into his holster. He looks at me and says, "Tonight's your lucky night, son. Be off with you."

SUPERLIE

It's four o'clock in the morning and all the cars in the city have gone home. Superman hovers outside the window of the bedroom. His cape is flapping like a red flag in the minty-fresh air. He's trying to open the window slowly to minimize the noise.

He glides in and lands with a gentle thud on the wooden laminate floor. He stares at Lois lying in the bed, curled up in a foeatal position with her back turned to him. He slowly unties his cape and pulls down his cherry-red underpants and peels off his skintight blue lycra Superman suit. He stands there with his bulging muscles silhouetted by lamplight streaming through the window. He shifts his considerable weight from one foot to the other, all the while staring at Lois. He gently lifts one corner of the blanket and tries to slip into the bed ever so discreetly.

Lois spins around and asks, "Where have you been?"

He fumbles for an answer. "Oh well, there was this meeting with the Justice League and the X-men and it just went on and on and on. You know how it is."

Lois turns her back on him and her body stutters with stifled sobs. All Superman can do is stare at a crack in the ceiling, rake his fingers through his hair and listen to the repetition of his heartbeats.

BABY

I stood at the bus stop in the bitter cold, waiting for the bus to my girlfriend's house. It was a day so cold that every breath made mini clouds of grey mist. It was also the day that I was going to take her to meet my mother for the very first time. I'd never taken a woman home to meet my mother before, because my mother was the type of mother who always said not to bring every woman I was with to meet her. She'd tell me to only bring the ones that I was serious about.

That's why I decided to introduce her to Sharon. Sharon was different from all the others, more mature and sexy like an older woman, even though she was younger than me. We clicked right away and I knew this woman could be my future. When I first raised the subject with Sharon, I tried to make it seem less serious than it obviously was by saying that we could go and check a movie – and then we could pop in to see my mum. She paused for just a moment and then smiled. Then she began to look a little nervous.

The number 3 bus finally came. I went upstairs, sat in the back seat, pulled out a book and began to read, hoping to pass the forty-five minute journey quickly. I began to feel like someone was staring at me and I looked up to see the bright hazel eyes of a little baby boy, with a little round face topped by a wisp of blond hair. At full height, standing on the seat in front of me, his head, arms and shoulders barely cleared the metal rail on top of the seat.

The baby smiled coyly at me and I smiled back, as you do. Suddenly the child dipped beneath the seat and reappeared, smiling. I smiled again, vaguely charmed by the kid's little game. He ducked beneath the seat and reappeared again with a shy laugh. I smiled. He did it again, and I laughed. He did it again and I laughed again. After ten minutes of this, I no longer found it even remotely amusing, though I smiled back politely every time. I tried reading, I tried looking out of the window, I tried cleaning my fingernails – anything so I wouldn't feel compelled to be locked into his little game. When I looked away, he shifted around in his seat trying to get into my line of sight. I could feel his beady little eyes on me, waiting for me to face him so that he could suck me into the game. The little bastard was absorbing all my energy, stopping me from reading my book, but too young for me to just tell him to fuck off and quit jerking my chain, tempting though that option was beginning to seem.

I looked around hopefully for his mother, but no one seemed quite near enough to him to be with him and no one seemed to be watching him, either, though several people seemed to be watching me.

I saw him out of the corner of my eye, dipping

beneath the seat and popping up again. I still smiled, just to be courteous. To be honest, this kid was really starting to piss me off, but I felt a bit guilty being angry with a baby. The child went on and on and I forced smile after irritated smile, trapped by this little shit.

Finally I gave up all pretence and just looked at the baby, stony-faced. Nothing stopped this child. He just continued bobbing up and down, laughing his damned fool head off. But after twenty minutes of this, it began to feel like he was laughing at me rather than laughing with me. His smile started to have a manic leery twist to it and his eyebrows began to arch.

He continued his little game, but each time he popped up he seemed to become just a little bit more hysterical. He began to throw back his head and point at me with his stubby little fingers. By this time, the whole bus was casting sidelong glances, no doubt wondering what I was doing to the poor child.

I was getting angry, really angry. At the same time, I couldn't believe that I was getting so pissed off with a little baby. But the angrier I got, the more hysterically he laughed, until he was laughing so much that he coughed and went bright red trying to catch his breath, just so he could laugh at me even harder. In the end, it was get off the bus or throttle the bastard, so I decided to jump off the bus a full three stops before I'd intended and walk the extra way to my girlfriend's house. As I rocketed down the stairs, I looked towards the back of the bus and, sure enough, he'd turned around and was still cackling and shaking his head. In frustrated defiance, I gave him the finger, but that only made him more animated in his hysteria. Even when I was outside on the pavement, looking up at the top windows, he was there drooling on the glass – and I was nearly a mile from Sharon's house in the bitter cold. I tried not to think that he'd won.

I arrived at her house feeling thoroughly cold, miserable and a bit shaken by my ordeal. I was distracted and a little impatient when she answered the door. "Are you ready?" I asked her, stepping just inside the door.

"For the cinema or to meet your mother?" she replied.

"Both, I guess," I said, a little surprised by such a direct question.

"I know I'm ready for the cinema. I'm not so sure about meeting your mum."

"W-why?" Now I was really confused.

"I know introducing me to your family is a big step for us, but I'm not sure we're really ready. There are things you don't know about me," she said, looking away.

"Like what? Tell me, please. Nothing's going to change the way I feel about you, honey, you know that." For the first time in my life, I knew that was true.

"Well, you know I don't talk about myself much; you just don't know why. I suppose I should have told you sooner, but it never seemed the right time. You were bound to find out, I just hoped it wouldn't be this soon. But now... See, my sister's just this minute arrived from Brighton for the weekend. I wasn't expecting them until the morning. She lives in Brighton, see, and – so does my son." She looked at me with big eyes, holding her breath, waiting.

And that's when I heard it: the sound of an infant's hysterical cynical laughter rippling in waves from the kitchen, the same sound that had been ringing in my ears for the last twenty minutes as I walked through the bitter cold.

JOB

"What the hell happened to your eyes, Frank? Don't tell me you've started wearing tinted contact lenses."

Frank turned to me and gave a wry half-smile, a smile I'd come to know over the years as the Feel Bad Smile.

I had known Frank for ten years. As the only two black guys living in halls at Loughborough University, I guess it was inevitable that Frank and I would become friends – that and the fact that the housing officer had assigned us as room-mates. Our building housed all the Chinese, Bangladeshi and Malaysian students and became commonly known throughout the school as the "ghetto".

The first time I saw the Feel Bad Smile, we were in the second year, and I went to the student union cafe for some coffee. Frank was already there, sitting with some of his teammates from the rugby squad. As I stirred the milk and sugar into my coffee, one of the guys tossed back his mousy hair, looked at Frank with a sly smile and asked, "So, guys, how's life in the ghetto?"

The entire table exploded with a roar of laughter. I got up immediately and walked towards the door, leaving my milky coffee still spiralling in a mini whirlpool in its styrofoam cup. I looked back, to see

Frank still sitting there with his head slightly stooped, looking up at me, wearing the Feel Bad Smile and trying to laugh along with the guys.

The second time I saw it was the day we met his girlfriend's father, who'd driven up from Surrey for the weekend. He stared at us, raising his blond bushy eyebrows as though we were of particular anthropological interest and said quite seriously, "You boys look like you've just stepped out of a vat of chocolate."

Even Frank's girlfriend laughed so hard she couldn't catch her breath. I walked away fast, hoping I'd keep from smacking the pair of them. Again, I left alone. When I looked back Frank was still standing between them, wearing the Feel Bad Smile.

But that was back in university. We stayed in touch after graduation, then, three or four years ago, found ourselves working for the same investment firm. In all the years that I'd known him, Frank's eyes had been dark brown, like mine, but suddenly I noticed that there were subtle pools of green that just weren't there before.

"Frank, how come your eyes are that colour?" I asked.

He flashed the Feel Bad Smile and said that his supervisor had him doing so much photocopying that the bright lights of the photocopier had bleached his pupils to a murky green colour.

"Oh my God! Why don't you complain to your

area manager or to the union rep?" I didn't know which was harder to believe – that a photocopier could bleach eye colour, or that Frank would put up with such disfigurement without so much as a single complaint.

He said he didn't want to kick up too much of a fuss, that he really needed to do well in this job. He was afraid if he complained, he'd get the sack. "I'm the only one in my family who's got a degree, the only one who's got a job like this. Look around, John. You and I are the only black guys in this company. I don't want to cause any trouble."

"But your eyes are green! How much are you willing to sacrifice for this damned job?" I couldn't believe what I was hearing.

"John, if your parents had never made sacrifices, you wouldn't be where you are now." He gesticulated urgently with his hands, his forehead pinched.

"Sure, but to them, the whole point of making those sacrifices was so that their kids wouldn't have to suffer like they did. You have to draw a line somewhere, man."

"Yeah, but have you ever read *She Stoops to Conquer*? Sometimes you have to suffer to succeed." He wouldn't look at me and rubbed a little groove into the wooden cafeteria table with his thumbnail.

"Have you ever read *Uncle Tom's Cabin*?" I nearly bellowed.

"With that attitude you'll never get promoted," he said quietly, almost like a mantra.

"If that's what getting promoted takes, I'll pass, thanks."

One Saturday afternoon, about a month later, the doorbell rang. It was Frank, holding a messy-looking box of stuff.

"John, you have to help me," he said, breathless for some reason. "The area manager is coming round for dinner. It's supposed to be a social visit, but I'm hoping he wants to talk about opportunities for promotion. Can I store this stuff at your house for a while?"

"What's in the box? Drugs? Porn? Groceries?" I had no idea what he was talking about.

"Just stuff I don't want the area manager to see." There was the Feel Bad Smile again, this time directed at my feet.

"Like what?"

"Like afro combs, cocoa butter, *Ebony* magazines, Marvin Gaye CDs – that sort of stuff. Can I leave it here?"

"Sure." What else could I say? "By the way, what the hell happened to your hair?"

"They installed new overhead lighting in the office to make us all more effective workers, something about repetitive pulses and biorhythms. I guess the light reacts weirdly with my hair and it's bleaching it blond."

"Why don't you just ask for a regular light, or a desk somewhere else?"

"I don't want it to seem like I'm not a team player. It's important that I don't make waves just now. See, I've got this plan to end up running this company, and it's working already. After this dinner I'm sure I'll have the promotion in the bag. Then you'll see. Eventually I'll be Chairman of the Board. Its first black chairman. Anyway, I've got to rush – the deli closes at five and I need spinach for the hors d'oevres and they've got a great selection of Bordeaux at the moment. Thanks for hanging onto that box for me." And he was gone, seeming not to notice that I was just standing there with my jaw hanging open, his box of shit threatening to slip out of my hands.

I didn't see Frank for a few days, it was Friday morning before I caught up with him in the corridor at work.

"So how did your big wing-ding dinner go?"

"It was great, man. I'm on my way up. Sheridan said he'd seen me grow and change since I joined the company. If I prove myself with the end of year report for our section, the promotion is mine. See, I told you, John, I'm moving up in the world. You wait – ten, fifteen years, this whole company will be mine."

"And when's that report due?" I kept trying to catch his eye, but he didn't seem to stand still long enough.

"Uh, Tuesday."

"What? Surely you can't do a whole section report

in just four days, all by yourself. It would take most people a month at the very least."

He looked proud when he squared his shoulders. "That's why I don't intend to sleep until it's over. I've been working on it since Monday, and I'm doing fine." Now that he mentioned it, he looked jangled and jumpy. I wondered if it was just Pro-Plus and coffee making him chew his lips and gesticulate more than usual.

I grabbed his arm and said, "Jesus, man, don't kill yourself like this. It's just a job."

"You see? That's why I'm up for promotion and you're not."

He had a point, I just wasn't sure it was the one he thought.

I came in on Monday morning and Frank was in exactly the same position as I'd seen him in when I left on Friday night. I'd offered to help him out over the weekend, but he'd barked, "I'm in control. I can do it. You just go enjoy your weekend." Like even having a weekend was for pansies and losers. So I left him to it.

Now I wish I hadn't been so quick to exit. He was a mess, slurring his words and fumbling with the keyboard on his computer like his hands were suddenly too large. He had dark circles around his eyes, and reeked of nasty coffee, way too many cigarettes, and stale sweat. Again, I offered to help, even just to clean up the office a bit, but he ordered me out by slurring and swearing at the same time. If he weren't my oldest friend, I might have laughed, or told him to fuck off.

On Tuesday morning, he stumbled over to my desk, loose-limbed and groggy, and whispered, "It's finished, John. Could you come down to reprographics with me to help me print it out? I know I've been an asshole, but I'm so shattered, I don't trust myself to do it right. I don't want to make any mistakes and I might press the wrong button or something. It's due in an hour. Please!"

Frank was so weak he could barely walk down the corridor without my help. Somehow we made it to reprographics, where one of the repro guys showed me what to do. I put in the disk which held the famous report. Frank sat in a shivering huddle on a stool in the corner.

"How many copies do you need?" I asked.

He mumbled a faintly whispered, "Ten."

"Let's see now, ten copies of two hundred pages. Here we go, press PRINT."

Suddenly, the moment I pressed the print button, John started to twitch and thrash as if he were plugged into the mains. His green eyes snapped wide open and his hands flew up in front of him, jerking about wildly. His blonde afro stood on end. At first I thought he was having some sort of seizure, brought on by the stress and weird lights and shit. Then I noticed his skin coming up in blotches. I swear, it looked like every word being printed was sucking a corresponding chunk of pigment from his skin. I just stood there stupidly for what seemed like hours, though it was probably no more than a minute. I couldn't seem to take in the horror that was right before me, as each printed page seemed to drain more and more of his colour. Finally, I rushed over to the machine, jabbing wildly at the console to stop the print run and hopefully save what little melanin he had left. But Frank shouted, obviously in agony, "NOOO! Get – the report – printed! It's due – in half an – hour. Can't fail – now."

All I could do was look on, horrified, as he contorted with pain for another ten minutes, and try to keep him from banging into things and doing more damage than absolutely necessary. Crazy. After the last page was printed, he lay gasping on the ground. Every last drop of colour had drained away and he was left looking like an albino, and a rather sickly albino at that. He stretched out his pasty hand to me and croaked, "Where are the reports?"

I lay them on the floor next to him and watched as he slowly curled around them, then levered himself upright, with the reports clutched to his chest. One more time, he flashed the Feel Bad Smile, and stumbled, tripped and crawled to the area manager's office.

I walked out of that building and never went back. I never saw Frank again, though I think about him all the time. After what I'd seen, what he'd done, I just couldn't bring myself to pick up the phone or make the short trip from my house to his. Somewhere in the loft I still have that box of his stuff. I can't bring myself to unpack it or throw it away.

STAG NIGHT

I told the guys that I didn't even want a stag night. To be quite honest, I was always the odd one out from the guys I'd hang out with. There were many times when I'd be stuck in the car driving around amongst the smell of cigarettes and beer. What I really wanted to do was to be curl up in bed watching late-night black-and-white love movies with a mug of hot cocoa and some digestive biscuits. Of course if I was to tell them that they'd probably wet themselves with laughter.

I realised that all groups of guys who hang around always have someone like me someone who just isn't macho. They needed a guy like me around to emphasise how macho they are and guys like me need guys like them to make up for the masculinity we think we lack. So in a strange way I guess we sort of needed each other. There'd be times when we'd meet up with other bunches of guys and I'd spot the guy exactly like me. While all the other guys were talking about all the girls they want to get with in the spot, we'd be talking about how cool Barbara Streisand was in *Yentl* and that we couldn't believe that hardly any of those tunes made it onto her greatest hits album.

The guys also claimed to know everything about everything, even if you didn't ask them. There was this one time when I broke up with my ex-girlfriend Lisa Anne, or I should say when she broke up with me, and I mistakenly went to the guys for advice. John, the largest of them at over six-foot-five and two hundred and forty pounds of pure muscle, and the expert on girls in the group because he'd had so many, looked at me with one raised eyebrow and said, "You know what your problem is, Roland?"

"No, what?"

"You give too much. You just plain old give too much. You're always telling a girlfriend exactly how you feel and about how much you love her. You make women over value their goods, and ultimately they start thinking that they're too good for you. All this honesty and adoration that you pour all over them make them start looking somewhere else for a challenge. Now take a look at me – I'm not the most handsome man in the world but I always have rich beautiful women and not once has a woman ever broken up with me. You know why?" he asked.

"Why?" I asked, knowing full well that he was going to tell me no matter what.

"Because the only way to keep a woman is to give them lots and lots of trouble."

"What?" I said incredulously.

"Believe me, it's true. Let me tell you why. If a woman doesn't know what your next move is going to be she will always be slightly mystified by you and that keeps her interested. It's a personal affront to her self-esteem that you're not in awe of her, so she'll be trying all the time to find out where you're coming from. She'll ring up and leave messages, send you notes, buy you gifts, as long as she's slightly unsure of your devotion. Then what you do is tell her only once that you love her. That night, treat her like a queen. She'll be overjoyed because for so long she'll have been working towards this point. The next day, take everything back to square one and pretend like you never said it. I guarantee you that she'll spend the rest of her life trying to get back to that point. You'll have her for life, and she'll do anything to be on your good side." Four other guys at the table nodded their heads approvingly.

I remember sitting there and thinking how fundamentally different I was from these guys. I mean, their perfect woman would wear tight miniskirts, high heels and have long hair and breast implants. My perfect woman would have short hair, a quirky face with no make-up, baggy clothes and sneakers. Their idea of a perfect night would be a smoky club and getting off with any skinny woman in tight clothes, with a minimum of conversation. My perfect night would be to watch *The Bridges of Madison County* while being hugged by my girlfriend and eating vanilla Haagen Dazs ice cream.

When I found the love of my life, Leone, who accepted me just for me, I began to drift slowly away from the guys. Leone thought that it was still good for me to have guy friends so she used to encourage me to go out with them. Then when Leone and I decided to get married I told the guys.

John looked at me and said, "Are you sure you're doing the right thing?"

"Of course I'm sure. What the hell kind of question is that? Isn't anybody going to congratulate me?"

Then all the guys told me congratulations, but none of them seemed to be smiling. I think somewhere in their minds they thought that they might not see me again, that this was the end. In my mind our friendship was coming to an end when I decided to marry Leone. I mean, Leone and I, we were perfect for each other – I could be myself. But the guys always wanted me to be something that I wasn't.

Then a week later I got a phone call from John saying that they were going to organise my stag night, that it would be the wildest stag night in human history. I pleaded with them. I begged them not to arrange a stag night and said that I really wasn't into things like that. They just said that I owed it to them to have a stag night and that the arrangements had already been made so I had to come. Leone thought it was a good idea, "After all," she said, "I am taking you away from them. I mean that before me they were your best friends." So I agreed to go, with the encouragement of Leone. This was sort of a going away party from the guys, even though a stag night organised by the most testosterone-saturated men in history made me pretty nervous.

Finally the night came. They beeped the horn and I kissed Leone and told her jokingly if I wasn't back in three days to call the police. I walked slowly towards the car feeling like a condemned man. I sat in the car, squashed in the centre of the backseat as usual. John turned around to me from the driver's seat and stared at me for a second, then he said, "Roland James, are you ready to go to – Amsterdam?"

As they all burst out with an energetic, "yes", as they burst poppers and blew party whistles and wore cone-shaped party hats that said 'STAG NIGHT' on them like it was some demented New Year's celebration, I held my head in my hands, and thought that I just knew this was going to be disastrous.

The guys led me around handcuffed, with a leather collar and chain around my neck. We crossed a small cobbled bridge that led you straight into the heart of Amsterdam's red-light district. I tried to explain to them that I wasn't like them. I wasn't not into drinking and loads of women, why didn't they just get it, but they just said that night I didn't have a choice.

The first place they took me to was one of the weed cafes, where they had a wide selection. Smoking marijuana in Amsterdam iss legal. This cafe had weed from Morocco to Mozambique, from Jamaica to Japan. The guys sat me down at a table and said, "Alright, Roland, this is your last night to drink some alcohol and smoke some weed and get some women with the boys, because in two days you, my friend, will be married and it'll all be over."

"Come on, guys, you know I don't smoke weed or drink and I ain't interested in no other woman except for my fiancée."

"Well there's no better time to start than now."

He began to line up a series of ten tequila slammers, and all ten of the guys started chanting, "Drink, drink, drink, drink, drink, drink, drink, drink, drink!

John looked at me and said, "Roland, are you ready?" as if he was introducing a world heavyweight title bout.

I looked at all of them and said, "You're not going to get me to drink, you guys know I don't drink."

"Well you got two ways that you can do this: you can either do it on you own or we can pull back your head and hold your nose and just pour it down your throat. So what will it be, are you gonna be a man for once in your life, huuuh?" As all of them stared down at me menacingly.

Now, I don't know what it was. Maybe it was the option of going along with it, was a tad more palatable than being forced, or maybe my masculinity or self-esteem rating was very low and this would boost it. Maybe I just wanted the whole thing to be over with as soon as possible, or maybe somewhere, deep down a part of me was really curious about getting high, or maybe it was peer pressure or testosterone pressure or a combination of all of these that made me say, "Alright, lets do this!"

The guys all gave a simultaneous roar and John immediately grabbed hold of one of the tiny glasses full of tequila and shouted, "One, two, three – go!" and banged it on the table and straight to my mouth. I swallowed it in one. I could feel it going down my throat and burning my chest like I'd swallowed a glassful of lava. Apart from a slightly short-of-breath feeling it wasn't too bad, but before I could catch my breath again I heard John saying, "One, two, three – go!"

Six tequila slammers later, I couldn't pronounce my words properly. After ten tequila slammers I was singing 'Love on the Rocks' by Neil Diamond and talking about how we had to go looking for Tracy Chapman because who knows where she disappeared to, and how she might be in Amsterdam. After fifteen tequila slammers I stepped up onto a table and tried to take off my shirt – with much difficulty because of my handcuffs. I then shouted to the entire cafe that all the drinks and weed for everyone was on me. At which point the guys pulled me down back into the chair. I couldn't remember any of these things, when I saw the videotape they'd made of the whole event. The first thing that I remembered was looking down into a toilet bowl and watching the inside of my guts flush away. After that it was like somebody had scraped away the hazy cobwebs of drunkenness, so I felt closer to sober than drunk. I walked back out to the cafe, a little weaker but surviving the ordeal. I asked one of the guys to get me a coffee, and with every sip I felt myself coming back to normal. The guys were congratulating me, like I was a part of a special club that I had never belonged to before. Halfway through my coffee John said, "Are you ready for some weed with your coffee?"

"C'mon, John, you have to be kidding. I can't smoke – I've got asthma. I want to be able to live long enough to get to my wedding. If I get an asthma attack I'll die. You fools wouldn't even know what to do. I don't even have my inhaler with me."

"OK, OK, stop whinging like an old woman for God's sake. Look, you don't have to smoke it, you could eat it."

"Eat it?"

"Yes, eat it. We could have them put it in a cheese sandwich for you or something. It's supposed to be good for you when you eat it. It helps to cure glaucoma."

"But I don't have glaucoma!"

"It's good for asthma, too," as they bought the sandwich to the table. Then John started singing. "Just eat it, eat it" to the tune of Michael Jackson's "Beat It", and all the guys joined in. Then I said, "Alright, alright I'll do it, just stop singing."

It didn't taste too bad with the weed in it. I finished the whole thing, and then they bought me another one. After I ate that I still didn't feel too bad, then I felt that I wanted to go to the toilet, but I couldn't be bothered to get up and walk there.

Suddenly, I had five different ideas, simultaneously, for lyrics of songs in the style of Burt Bacharach. I thought that I should get up right now and get a pen and paper and write it all down in case I forgot, but then I couldn't be bothered. A little after that, heavy paranoia began to set in. I kept feeling that everyone was watching me, not just the guys but also everyone in the cafe. I had the feeling that they were all talking about me and laughing. I thought they were all laughing because they'd all slept with my fiancée, and I didn't know. The guys especially were looking right at me and laughing, so I thought I'd just look to my right so they wouldn't know that I was onto them. So the guys started to look to my right to see what I was looking at, but I thought that they were trying to copy my movements. So I quickly looked to the left, so I could trip them up. The next thing I knew was that I began to see every detail in things. There was a tiny knothole, no bigger than the size of a twenty pence piece, in the door to the toilet. So I thought that there was somebody watching me through that hole every time I looked. I spent the next half an hour trying to turn my head quickly, so I could catch the person looking at me through the hole. I must have flicked my head in that direction about forty times. After about an hour I began to lose that paranoid feeling and my head began to clear.

John signalled to the guys for us to leave. They pulled me by my handcuffs out of the cafe and onto the streets. We walked past the red-lit windows, where the prostitutes cut sharp silhouettes in the gleam of their red-lit glass booths. In each booth women like shop mannequins struck poses displaying their bodies all clad in PVC thigh-length boots with sharp stiletto heels.

I told them, "Listen, guys, getting me to smoke and drink is one thing, but me and a prostitute is something completely different. If I'm smoking and drinking I'm only hurting myself, but if I sleep with a prostitute I'm be hurting my fiancée. I am really not down with this!"

"What are you talking about? How is she going to find out?" John fired back.

"You see you just don't get it, do you. I will know, I'll feel bad because I've betrayed her."

"Look, we've already paid so you have to do it."

"Then I'll give you back your money. There's no way that this is going to happen."

John kept pulling me through the cobbled streets, by the handcuffs. We weaved our way in between hundreds of men with a swagger in their walk, and a lecherous look in their eyes.

After we turned on to the second alleyway I came to an abrupt halt. John asked what was the matter. I began to squint to get a clearer view. Right there in front of me, in one of those dim red-lit booths, was my Aunt Janet. I fell to the ground in weak disbelief and held my head, thinking to myself that I had heard that she went to Europe to be a dancer but this I just could not believe. I looked again at my poor Aunt Janet. She was all trussed up in PVC bra and panties with a leather whip in her left hand, knocking on her glass to attract passers-by. The guys all stooped down towards me, wondering what was wrong. I told them that the woman in the booth was my aunt who used to baby-sit for me when I was a kid. I said to John with tears in my voice, "If she needed help she could have come to me. I'd have helped her. I'd have done anything to prevent this, she could have stayed at my flat, and I would've found her a job."

Then John said, "Alright, that's it! We're not leaving Roland's aunt here. Everyone get out all your money and your credit cards we're going to buy her a plane ticket home and we'll all help to find her a job."

And then all the guys started handing John all their money, and credit cards. I began to walk towards the booth, and she was jogging on the spot and blowing into her hands to warm herself. I walked slowly towards her. She opened her window having not recognised me, and shouted, "Cheap price for you!"

And it was then that I realised that it wasn't her. It was somebody else's Aunt Janet. I walked back to the guys and told them. They all seemed sad. They took the handcuffs and the leather chain off. John put his arm round my shoulder and we walked back to the hotel in silence, and we sat in my room talking about stories about our families. I learned a lot about the guys that night and we still remained friends.

SEX ED

First of all, I have to hand it to my father. I mean, it couldn't have been easy for him. I'm sure his father never told him, but maybe that was the reason he was telling me. I remember that morning very clearly. It was the end of the summer when I was ten years old. I was outside playing marbles, or killing wasps, like I did just about every day during that summer.

My father called out to me in the Serious Tone. Now, the Serious Tone up till that point meant only one thing: that I was in a whole lot of serious trouble. My mind started skipping over everything I could possibly have done wrong, so I'd be ready with a suitable excuse. I couldn't think of a single thing, so I ran upstairs with a sheepish look, in the hope that I might convey from the very beginning the heartfelt sorrow I truly felt for whatever it was I'd done wrong.

When I got upstairs, I found my father in the bedroom, holding a pointer stick in front of a big flip-top book which was propped against the wall. It looked like there were at least a dozen charts with diagrams of various parts of the human body in bright blues and yellows. He told me to sit down, that he wanted to talk to me. As a relatively obedient child, I sat in front of the mysterious pictures with my hands on my knees. He asked me if I knew where babies come from.

"Um – mumblemumblemumble – sort of –" I said, feeling mortified and very brave at the same time.

"What? Speak up, son."

I answered with my ten-year-old's knowledge. "Well, I know they come from the mother's belly, but I don't know how they get in there or anything."

Even at that young age, I craved information and now that he'd raised the subject I was quite interested to find out. Until that moment, it had never occurred to me to ask about the mechanics of how babies were made. I was too busy playing marbles and reading Richie Rich comics, I guess.

He pointed to the diagram of a woman's womb and showed where male sperm travelled to meet the female egg. Then he told me that these would meet to form a baby, and that it would take nine months to grow inside the woman's womb. The baby would then be born through the mother's vagina. Fair enough. Then came the tricky part. I asked my poor father, "So, how does the sperm get inside the womb?"

My father began to stutter. I could tell from his eyes that he was deciding what he should leave out. He flipped the pages of the diagram book clumsily. He came to the stylised picture of a bright-blue penis with a yellow scrotum and urethra. He said the sperm came from the penis. Now, this whole conversation was beginning to blow my mind, because even at ten

I knew I had one of those penis things, even though mine wasn't bright-blue and yellow.

My father continued by saying that when the penis is ready it is inserted into the vagina.

Like any good ten-year-old, I asked, "So, how do you know when it's ready?"

He started umming and ahhing. Finally, he used his bent index finger to illustrate. "Well, you see, son, the penis is usually soft, but when it's, ah, ready, it becomes hard and stands up straight. That's called an erection." He slowly straightened his index finger out. Without looking up from his demonstration, he asked if I understood.

I said, "Yes."

He said, "Any questions?"

I said, "No."

"OK, you can go now." I noticed that his armpits were soaked with sweat, as if he'd been through some terrible ordeal and escaped by a very narrow margin. He smiled and seemed very pleased.

As far as I knew, I had never had an erection, which meant I was obviously not "ready". This in turn meant that, until I was ready, this conversation had absolutely nothing to do with me. It never occurred to me that I'd once been the baby in those diagrams, and when it finally did, it wasn't a particularly interesting revelation. As soon as my father told me I could go, I promptly filed away the whole talk under "weird grown-up things" and picked up an *Archie* comic I'd brought in with me. As my father shuffled his charts and put away his pointing stick, he seemed to stare at me for a while, making sure that I was alright. I had no idea why, and I certainly had no idea that this was the beginning of a very turbulent year.

Two weeks later, school started again and things started getting a little weird. Suddenly, during every recess, it seemed that all the boys who used to play marbles with me had found something new to amuse them. They could usually be found hovering around the door to the art supplies storeroom at the back of our classroom. Apparently the four girls in our class who already had protruding breasts put on a daily show in there at break time. They chose a few boys to lock themselves in with and they'd then strip off their blouses to show off their new-found bosoms, much to the delight of the chosen few.

Naturally, soon enough, boys would gather every day in front of the door hoping to be selected. The boys who went in came out somehow different. Pastimes like marbles and football cards, which were the centre of my world, seemed to become meaningless to the chosen boys. In fact, having been in with the girls made them queue up all the more hopefully in the days that followed – they were no longer there out of curiosity, but out of downright desperation.

At first, I stood outside the door as a complete opportunist, trying to convince boys who didn't want their marbles or football cards to give them to me. I was sure that this breast thing was a fad. When the other boys finally saw sense, they'd go back to playing proper games and I'd be there with more marbles and cards than I could carry.

After about a week of hustling outside the storeroom door I became a little curious, I guess. That's how I became part of the crowd that waited outside to be chosen. The thought of seeing girls from my own class naked wasn't even a particularly exciting notion to me. I think the exciting part was waiting everyday to see if I would be one of the boys picked that day.

By November, after two months of standing outside that door, I still had never been picked. Some guys were being picked four or five times. But I also noticed that there were three other guys besides me who weren't ever chosen. After a while we all sort of realised that we were never going to be picked, so we started hanging out with each other instead. Those boys became my first posse of friends – the reject posse.

From that point on, every break time found the reject posse hanging-out under a tree in the schoolyard instead of facing the rejection. Don't get me wrong, the guys in the reject posse were by no means ugly or nerds, we were just all very dark-skinned, something that didn't win you points in primary school.

We hung out and played together. We ate lunch together, wandered around the school together. We formed our own secret language and didn't mix much with the other kids. We were also the first to bring skateboards to school and we could do all the hardest tricks. All of a sudden, the reject posse became the coolest shit in primary school.

And the strangest thing happened. The stripper girls from the art room made an open invitation to the reject posse to attend one of their notorious shows. But by this time, we figured we were too cool for all that. We also already had all the other guys' marbles, just waiting for the interest in the stripper girls to wane, and it seemed that if we refused them, the process just might be speeded up.

There are two things I should probably say at this point. First, I still had no clue that my father's lecture about where babies came from had anything to do with boys lining up to see girls take their clothes off. Second, the group decision that the reject posse made was, in retrospect, probably the beginning of a disturbing trend in my life to, when pressed, choose hanging out with the guys over sex.

About six months on from this time a really strange thing happened. It was during that summer that was so hot that glassy waves of heat rose from the ground and there was a constant shortage of water. I was sweating so much that I'd be in the bathroom for as long as there was water, trying to wash away the hot uncomfortable stickiness of sweat. It was during one of my multiple bathroom trips that the strangest of things occurred. I was soaping my legs and sliding them against each other while listening to Cyndi Lauper's song "Girls Just Wanna Have Fun" on the radio. As I danced I felt something shifting within me, as if I was on the downside of a roller coaster. I couldn't bring myself to stop. After two more, similar up-tempo songs I could feel my whole body tense with extreme pleasure as I closed my eyes. I opened my eyes one by one to see if I was still alive, and I was. Everything I saw around me seemed to look overly defined. The light in the bathroom seemed extra bright; the water pressure in the shower seemed unusually high. I could even hear all the percussion in the songs playing on the radio. I didn't know it then but I had just had my first orgasm.

I stood still in the shower confounded by the extreme feeling of what had just happened. Then in a moment of extreme paranoia I began looking all around to see if there were hidden cameras looking in on me. I then slowly reached out my hand for the soap and started making another thick soapy lather between my thighs and tried to get the same sliding leg action to see if it would happen again, and it did. It took a little while longer but it happened. After the fifteenth time I was beginning to feel a bit weak. I felt my knees beginning to buckle and people kept knocking on the door wanting to use the toilet. The rest of the day I just lay in bed wondering what the hell that was all about, but thinking that whatever it was I couldn't wait to do it again.

At this juncture I should probably say a few things. The first is that I had no clue about what masturbation was, because if anybody else knew they certainly didn't tell me. The second is that I had these orgasms without an erection and also without any messy wet stuff usually associated with orgasms. The third is that I had not even an inkling that the lecture from my father on how babies were made, had anything to do with the episode in the bathroom. My father talked about the mechanics of baby making, but never mentioned how much incredible fun you could have all on your lonesome. It seemed quite clear to me from my father's talk that if people wanted babies they would have sex. What was not clear was that sex gave you this groovy feeling, and that in repeated attempts to get to this groovy feeling people would fuck-up and then a baby would be made.

All the above reasons, and my increasingly bizarre eleven-year-old's existential worldview, led me to believe the following: I had invented what happened in the bathroom. I thought that I had invented masturbation. I also never told any of my friends about it because in a selfish way I didn't want anybody else to be able to do it. As far as I was concerned I'd invented it and I was going to keep it for myself. So as a result I became the cleanest eleven-year-old in living history, bathing three, sometimes four, times a day. Our water bill nearly doubled. My father asked me why the hell I was bathing so much.

Now, there are certain things that happen when you think that you have invented masturbation. One of them is that you find new and more novel ways to do it. The bedroom could replace the bathroom and skin cream could replace soap, and so on. There was no blueprint that I knew of so, like a brilliant experimental artist, I was free to create and stretch the form beyond what little I already knew.

A couple of months later we were whisked away to Barbados on holiday. But not just my immediate family; my two uncles, three aunts and their five children came, along with three other cousins whom I'd never met in my life. My grandma paid for them because their parents could never afford to take them on holiday. My parents rented a five-bedroom guesthouse and all the cousins had to sleep in one room with two king-size beds. All the younger cousins shared one bed, all lined up width-wise like sardines. Ian and I, being the tallest and the oldest, shared the other bed. His mum and mine were twins and we were also the same age. We saw each other often so we were a lot closer than cousins. I often thought of him as my brother. So we were glad that we had a bed to ourselves. That night I was having problems getting to sleep, probably because of jet lag. My cousin and I were lying down with our backs facing each other. Slowly I could feel the mattress undulating and then rapidly it began to pick up pace and vigour. I turned around slowly to see what he was doing and he must have felt me turn around because he immediately stopped. Then there wasn't a movement from him; it didn't even sound like he was breathing. So I pretended I was just changing position and continued to breathe deeply to make him think I was still asleep. Slowly he began again. I sprang up and whispered, "What are you doing?"

"Nothing," he whispered back immediately.

There was a long pause and then I whispered, "Are you doing that thing that gives you a weird feeling in your dick."

He turned around and whispered, "How do you know about that?"

"Because I do it too."

"Really?"

"Yeah."

He paused for a while then asked, "How long have you been doing it?"

"A couple of months," I said

"Me too. What naked ladies do you look at?"

"Naked ladies?"

"Yeah. What naked ladies do you look at? What magazines?"

"I ain't never done it and looked at no naked ladies," I said, and he looked at me confused.

Now, before this point it had never dawned on me that what I was doing was connected with women in general. I was just going for the sort of groovy feel of it all, but my cousin, he knew it all. He was experienced, and he was a professional. He handed me a copy of *Hustler* magazine and said, "here, take a look." I turned the pages but it was way too dark to see anything.

"It's too dark I can't see anything."

He turned to me and gave me a small penlight. At that point I thought, damn, he's got skills. Then he asked me which hand I used most, the left hand or the right hand. "Hands? I don't use any hands, I just sort of rub my legs together and it happens," I said.

"Really, wow. I think I'll try that." And then he started trying my style.

After about ten minutes he came to a dead stop and I asked, "Did it work?"

He said it didn't work he just got tired of trying, so he was going back to his way. So I decided to try his way, with the hand and the naked women and, I tell you, it was much more intense. I lay there thinking that this was some mind-blowing shit.

So when all our frantic activity had come to a halt, I asked him where or how might one procure such a fine publication? He told me that he got it from the local barber, who had hundreds, and every now and then, when the chance arose, he'd swipe one or two. So I decided immediately that as soon as I got home I was going to have a change of barber. For the next two years my hair was impeccably cut.

THIEF

Tonight is the night. I'm on my way to rob the house I've been staking-out now for over two months. Don't get me wrong. I do not approve of thieves or thieving, but I have been left with no choice. My mother desperately needs a heart transplant operation and there's no other way that I can afford it. I refuse to just sit here and watch my mother die when some fat cat is probably living high off ripping-off people like me. Everything in his house is probably insured for twice the amount it's worth anyway. Hell, I'm probably doing him a favour. I look up at the white six-foot wall and throw my climbing hook, pull my way up and straddle the top of the wall watching out for the five vicious security dogs that roam the grounds.

One day when I was surveying the house the paper delivery boy rode by and someone had left the security gates open. The five dobermans bolted out the gate like racing greyhounds and chased and chased the paper boy, who rode as quick as he could but even before he was out of sight they caught up with him cleverly threw him off balance and started savaging his legs. Finally, a passing car stopped and the driver started beeping his horn which startled the dogs for a moment and the driver pulled the boy inside the car.

The dogs, satisfied with their teamwork, trotted through the open gates back into the grounds.

Looking down on these dogs I see them baring their canines like polished ivory knives. I pull out my plastic bag and take out five defrosted t-bone steaks packed with sleeping pills. I drop them to the ground, one by one to make sure each dog eats his fill and five minutes later the once vicious dogs look like young pups asleep. I jump down into the grounds, careful not to step on the sleeping dogs, and make my way by sliding across the wall to the west side camera and cut the wires with pliers. I slide myself against the wall over to the east side cameras and cut the wires. I walk across the grounds until I reach the house, then from my bag I take out my climbing hook, throw it up to the roof and I begin pulling myself up to a window. I pull out my diamond cutter and cut a small circle in the glass, which I tap out. It barely makes a sound as it falls on to the carpet. I reach my hand in and unlock the window and climb inside the room. I switch on my *mag lite* torchlight and I start to make my way to the master bedroom, so I can get my hands on all their fine jewellery.

I take no more than two steps outside the room before I feel the chill of cold steel at the side of my head. I turn around slowly to face the silver barrel of a barretta. Holding it to my face is a skinny gangly-looking girl, about five-foot-two with a terribly acned face and thick glasses and stringy blonde hair down to her bony shoulders. I say to her, "Take it easy with that, you might make a mistake and blow my head off."

She says, "If I blow your head off believe me it won't be a mistake."

I say, "I've been watching this house for months, I've never seen you here."

She says "Unfortunately for you I only arrived today. This is my uncle's house and I'll be damned if I let you rob him."

"OK, fine, I'll just leave the way I came and we can forget the whole thing."

"Uh, uh, I don't think so. I think you'll wait here while I call the police." As she pulls out a mobile phone with her free hand and begins dialling.

I start to plead, "Look, please don't call the police. I'm not really a thief, this is the first time I've ever done something like this. Please you have to believe me!"

"Yeah, sure."

"Listen, little girl."

"I'm not a girl I'm a woman."

"Of course you're a woman. Look I'll do anything, just don't call the police."

"Take off your ski mask." I take off my ski mask and she stares at me and starts to smile and says, "Oh my, my, my, you wouldn't happen to have come here to try to rape me would you?"

"What! No, no, no, I don't want to rape anyone. Look, I'm just trying to get some money together so that my mother can have an important operation. If she doesn't get it, she'll die. I didn't come here to hurt or rape nobody."

"What's the matter? I ain't good enough for you to rape?"

"What the hell are you talking about I don't want to rape you?"

"For someone so good-looking you sure are dumb. Let me put it to you straight, this is how it is. Now I have two options: I could either blow your head off right here and say I shot an intruder, or we could have sex and I could let you go back to your ill mum."

"Come on, you have to be kidding? Look I'm leaving, if you're going to shoot me go ahead and shoot me."

She pulled back the trigger. "Don't test me. I'm a teenager and my hormones are all over the place. If you think I'm too ugly to have sex with I swear to God I'll shoot you right between the eyes."

"Look, you're not too ugly but – but – How old are you anyway?"

"I'll be sixteen next week."

"You're not even old enough. I can't do it it's against the law."

"Listen to me. You're a burglar, you're not in a position to debate points of law."

"Look, all I'm trying to do is get some money for my mother. She's at King George Hospital. You can ring them up to check. Her name is Margaret Jones. Please, she's all I have in this life!"

"OK, I'll cut you a deal. You have sex with me and I'll give you some money to take care of your mother. I've got a trust fund that I could take money from, OK."

As she begins taking down her skirt and panties with her free hand, the other hand still poised on the cocked trigger. Her body is all bones joined together at the joints. She's flat-chested and completely the oppposite of any woman I've ever been attracted to. "Come on already, take down you pants." I do it. She lies back on the bed in an extremely matter-of-fact, unsexy way. I try to think of every erotic scenario stored in my head to try and make myself sufficiently aroused. As I grab her by her skinny waist she says, "Wait I'm a virgin, so be careful and gentle."

"What? A virgin! Listen, are you sure you want to do this? Don't you think you should wait and do this with someone who's really special to you? I really don't think that I'm the one who should take your virginity. I mean, you don't even know me."

"Look, this is the one opportunity I have to lose my virginity with someone so handsome, and by God I'm taking it. I know I'm not very pretty. Nobody wants to be my boyfriend and I don't want to be a virgin forever. I'm the only virgin left in my class. I don't want to end up being a virgin into my forties, so this is it. So this is it!"

"Listen, all those girls in your class are lying. They're just saying that they've done it. Everyone says that when they're young."

"Kiss me. Kiss me all over my body." I pause. "Listen, kiss me or I'll kill you where you stand, Goddamit." As she takes aim with the gun.

I start gently kissing her milky-white stomach.

87

Her skin has the faint smell of sour milk but tastes sweet and dry, like baby powder. I have to convince myself that this is a beautiful sexy woman that I'm with. Her body starts trembling and I hope that she won't get too hot and squeeze the trigger of the gun by mistake. I kiss the side of her waist and move up her side to her ribs. I see every single rib and pass my tongue over them. She moans and pulls my head around to her pert young breast. She shouts, "Put it in now! Put it in now, I'm ready!" and I guide myself slooooowly into her.

With every push she cries out, not as if in pleasure but as if she's in terrible pain. I ask her, "Should I stop?"

"No keep on!"

"But it looks like you're in pain?"

"Keep on. Don't stop – do it!" I continue and she starts to work up a rhythm and starts smiling. As she puts her arms around me I can feel the heel of the gun in my spine. Her body begins to shudder and tense as she screams out and then falls back on the bed. She opens her eyes and curls into a little tiny ball and begins to cry.

"Are you alright?"

"Yes. Can I have a hug?" I put my arms around her tiny waist and cup my body around hers until her sobs eventually subside. She reaches into a drawer and pulls out a polaroid camera and cheque book. She turns around and snaps a picture of me.

"What are you doing?" I ask.

She stands up from the bed and blows on the polaroid and says, "You're going to come back to see me on Saturday night, or else I'll pop this picture straight down to the police station. OK?"

"Alright, alright."

"Heres a cheque for a thousand pounds for your mum." But before she gives me the cheque she says, "First you have to give me your phone number." As she snatches the cheque away before I can put my hands on it and throws a pen and some paper on the bed. "This better be the right number or else you'll be hearing from the police." Then she hands me the cheque.

I put on my clothes and say, "Can you put the dogs away when I leave?"

"Sure, as long as you kiss me before you go." I give her a half-hearted kiss as she pulls me tightly towards her and searches my mouth with her tongue for an intolerably long time. As our mouths part she says solemnly, "I love you." She walks me to the gate and says, "See you next week, honey."

I walk down the dark street looking for a cab, thinking about my mother and the cheque in my pocket.

TREE

"Good morning, darling," I said as I watched her stretch the yawned sleep out of her body. "Good morning, darling," I repeated, thinking that through yawning she may not have heard me.

She turned to me with a look that made me instinctively know that something serious was on her mind. I mean, the last time she looked at me like that was when she'd accidentally rolled over the cat with the car and she didn't know how to tell me. Only after the cat had been missing for a week and after I'd fly-posted five hundred pictures of the cat did she tell me, with the same expression she had right then. So I knew this was serious.

"What?" I asked. Receiving no answer, I asked again, "What's wrong with you?"

"Oh, nothing," she said.

"If it's nothing then why are you looking so worried? Did you have a bad dream or something?"

Susan was never the best of communicators. She had a tendency to keep things bottled up and, as if the pressure inside made the situation more concentrated and more dangerous, she would erupt like a volcano, spreading complete havoc and destruction. So I had become used to trying to coax these problems out of her when they were in their foetal stage, before they grew.

She said, "It's nothing, actually, uhh, uuhh, well, there is something. I don't know how to say this."

"What? Just say it, darling."

"You promise you won't get angry?"

"I promise. What is it?" Then there was an eerie contemplative silence, where she glanced slightly away to the side of the bed. I came round to the other side of the bed, to hold her hand and to make eye contact.

"I've been having an affair."

"You what!" I shouted, letting go of her hand, taking two stunned staggered steps backwards.

"You promised you wouldn't get angry," she whined.

"How in the hell could you not expect me to be angry over this?" As I paced nervously up and down the side of the bed, rubbing my temples 'cause I felt the most severe migraine of my life rising, like mercury in a thermometer, up my neck.

"But you promised!" she shrieked.

"I can't believe this shit. After all we've been through for two years. How can you do this to me? What did I do to you to cause this? I can't fucking believe this. How long has this been going on, huh-huh?"

"A year."

"A fucking year. What do you mean, a year? We've only been going out for two years. What are you saying? Let me get this right. So you're saying that fifty percent of this relationship has just been one big fucking lie. Is that what you're saying?"

By this time I was so shocked and disgusted with her I was facing the wall with my arms folded. Then something struck me as suddenly as the light of a bulb cuts the darkness in a room, and I turned to her as my disgust morphed into inquisitive finger-pointing venom.

"Hold on. You only moved in with me a little over a year ago. So what, you had an affair as soon as you moved in with me, huh-huh? C'mon, you at least owe me a fucking explanation. You at least owe me that. So who is it with, huh? Is it Colin? That fucking dog. I've never liked him!"

"It's not Colin," she mumbled, with her eyes staring everywhere but at me.

"Who is it then? Is it Frank. That sneaky little fuck!"

"No, it's not Frank. Look, it's not a guy, alright. Does that make you feel better?" she bellowed with mock indignation.

"Oh my God, you had an affair with a woman."

"Relax, it's not a woman either."

"Hold on. It's not a woman and it's not a man. What kind of fucking affair is this?"

"It's um – Well – uhh, it's a tree."

"A what?"

"A tree."

"A tree? As in with leaves and branches?"

"Yeah."

Well, to be honest I didn't know what to say. I didn't know whether to laugh or cry. I mean, what exactly are you supposed to say when your girlfriend has been having an affair with a tree for a year? I mean, a man, a woman, a transvestite or even a transsexual I could probably deal with. If the competitor was human, I could channel an adequate amount of hate towards the person for all their illicit phone calls, hidden meetings and general home-wrecking. But when a tree's been having relations with your girlfriend, you could never be quite sure what the appropriate reaction should be. Then I began to think, what kind of tree would she jeopardise our relationship for?

So I asked, "Hold on. Hold right on. Do I know this tree?"

"Yes. It's the big tree in the backyard."

I shouted in pure exasperation, "I can't believe it. I can't – that tree? I planted that fucking tree with my own bare hands. I remember that fucker when he was nothing but a damned sapling. I planted him myself about four years ago and this is how he repays me. I remember how many times I took my last money to buy fertiliser for that fuck, and this is how he pays me back, – by having an affair with my girlfriend? Hold on. There's something I don't understand. Where the hell did you get the time to have an affair? Answer me!"

"Don't make me go into this, please."

"Tell me!"

"All of this doesn't make any difference because I'm moving out today," she announced in a strongly defiant tone.

"Hold on, hold on, hold on. What? You're moving out? So after two years of going out, you're just going to leave. Just like that? You mean all the time we spent together counts for nothing? Susan, to be honest, I don't care whether you've had affair. We can get over this, please, let's talk. I ... I love you, Susan. Let's just talk."

"We don't have anything to talk about. At twelve o'clock some workmen are coming to build a tree house in the tree that's my lover, and I'm moving in there," she announced.

"What? You can't move in there!" I protested.

"Why?"

"Because it's my yard and my tree!"

"You see, that's exactly the reason I'm leaving you – because you're so fucking petty and selfish."

"Well, I may be petty and selfish, but the fact remains that it's still my yard and my tree."

"For your information, after one year of living together, I'm legally your common-law wife, so if you don't give me that land and that tree, I'm going to take you for half of everything you have. Half of your car, half of your house, half of your furniture. Believe me, you're getting off easy with me!"

With that she turned sharply, put on her jeans and a T-shirt and pulled out two pre-packed suitcases from the cupboard and stormed out the back door into the yard and sat on one of the tree's roots, with one hand curved halfway around its thick craggy trunk, her cheek pressed against its other side.

The workmen eventually came with all the materials for the tree house, plus windows, plumbing, electric wires and all the things for the modern comforts of a home. All day they were sawing and drilling, all supervised by Susan, whose face had a sickeningly contented smile the entire time. Finally, by about nine o'clock, it was all finished and the workmen left, and she moved into her new home and switched on her light.

That night I was so distraught. I tried to go to bed and sleep, just to stop thinking about it all the time, but I couldn't sleep. The whole thing was just running over and over again, like a rewound tape in my head. I mean, my life was a wreck. My girlfriend had been having an affair in my backyard with an oak tree, right under my nose. I tried to make some dinner but it tasted like shit, and I threw it away. She always used to cook. She would always know how much seasoning to put in food, how long to cook it for and what kind of salad would go well with it.

Then I thought, fuck it! I don't need her! And I decided to pull down the dusty old menu book my mother gave me when I moved into the flat. I thought to myself, even if it takes all night I'm going to cook something that's edible.

At around twelve o'clock, over a frustrating bowl of

over-cooked pasta, I saw her through my kitchen window in the yard. She stepped down the stairs of her tree house with just a towel wrapped around her, which she slowly unwrapped at the foot of the tree to reveal her plump firm curves., even more curvy now 'cause of their silhouette in the moonlight. She reached both her hands down and grabbed handfuls of dried leaves and started rubbing her face with them. Her eyes closed as she released the leaves, letting them slide down the contours of her naked body, like a shower. She started fondling her breasts as if she was trying to check the weight of them with her palms. I could see the mound of her stomach crease as she clumsily bent down and grabbed two more handfuls of dried leaves and caressed her thighs up and down with all the grace of a painter painting the final strokes of a picture.

Her knees buckled with pleasure as her waist began to automatically gyrate with heat. She grabbed up another handful of dried leaves and pressed them in between her legs, throwing her head back with pleasure and moaning at the stars. I thought to myself that she never ever got that wild with me at any time. I wanted to turn away but I couldn't. I just stood frozen at the kitchen window in the dark, watching her grabbing more dried leaves and smelling them and rubbing them over her chest. Then she dropped to her knees and took hold of a low, thick, protuberant knot in the truck with her two hands and began licking and kissing it with the vigour of a starving man attacking a ripe piece of fruit.

I couldn't take it, my heart was beating so loudly that my headache returned. I mean, I really couldn't tell what was worse: the fact that she was doing this or the fact that she was enjoying it so much. Then she pulled all of her naked one hundred and forty pounds up onto one of the low branches and straddled it like some Olympic athlete, while hugging and kissing the trunk. As she rode that low branch like an expert cowboy in a rodeo, it was bending to near breaking point under her weight. She was moaning so loudly that I could hear her clearly from the kitchen, and I could swear the breeze blowing through its leaves made a rustling creaking sound that made it seem like the tree was moaning back ... I couldn't watch anymore. I tried going to bed, but I couldn't sleep 'cause I could hear her moaning through the night. Every time I'd think it was over, five minutes later it would start up again.

The next morning I saw her going off to work, all bouncy and fresh with a big smile on her face as she walked through the garden gate. I don't know what happened, I'm not sure whether it was the smile on her face or my lack of sleep that made me snap. That morning I said to myself, that's it, I've had enough. No tree is going to make a fool of me, not in my own backyard. I went out straight to my local DIY store and bought a steely new buzz saw, came back home and ran into the yard in a fit of demented anger and sliced the blade's rotating chain into the thick base of the tree's trunk. I didn't stop until the splinters stopped flying.

As I looked at the fallen tree with its smashed tree house and all, I stood on the tree stump like a medal winner and shouted to the sky with the buzz saw held aloft, still roaring to the skies like some depraved murderer in a horror film shouting, "No tree can make a fool of me and live! Ha, ha, hahahahahaaaa!" As if that wasn't enough, I stepped down and hacked the fallen tree into many different sections to vent my anger further. Finally, my energy spent and the tree chopped up into hundreds of pieces, I went back into the house and tried to get some sleep.

I awoke to a blood-curdling scream. I rushed outside and shouted to her, "How do you like your precious tree now, huh-huh?" But she was too overcome by grief to even answer me. I felt bad seeing her curled up on the stump like an child, sobbing so hard. She cried a constant whining cry like a stray kitten that whole night, and after a while I was even beginning to get angry at the fact that she was so sad. She probably wouldn't have cried this much if I'd died. She really did love that tree, but it was obvious that she'd never loved me. Something in me wanted her to hurt even more. Hurt with the kind of jealous pain I was feeling.

So the next morning while she still lay there sniffling, I went to my local greengrocer and bought a big ripe watermelon, took it home, drilled a hole in it and took it into the garden where I proceeded to try and fuck it to try and make her jealous. She just looked at me and shouted, "You pervert!" and packed her suitcases with the strewn remains of the chopped-up tree and left.

BLADE

Due to a strange intersection of events in my life, I'd come to rely on picking up hitch-hiking strangers on the highway to satisfy my unusual sexual needs. More often than not, I managed to seduce them. The trouble was that while I was making love I needed to see some blood, so I had to pull out a blade. Now, don't get me wrong, I never intended to hurt them. All I wanted was to see a little blood. But women are so squeamish these days, they don't seem to understand my situation. As soon as I pulled out my butcher's knife, they got all hysterical and started screaming and trying to run away. Now, if they'd just relaxed, all they'd have left with was a slight flesh wound and a new sexual experience.

Of course it never went that smoothly. Once they'd seen the knife, I usually ended up cutting them a lot deeper than I meant to, due to their ridiculous thrashing around and trying to escape, and unfortunately sometimes they died. Alright, in fact all of them died, but I swear killing them was never ever part of my plan when I picked them up. It was really not my fault, I mean, anybody could end up like me. Even you. Don't believe me? Listen to this, and I'll ask you again.

When I was young, my father owned the main supplier for all the butchers in the south east. We had the biggest meat storage and shipping facility in the country, including a vast warehouse of meat ready to be despatched. Every summer holiday from the time I was eleven, I helped out at the warehouse. I became accustomed to the blood and skin of dead animals quite quickly. It was my job to clean out the lockers in the warehouse and sometimes, if it was a quiet day and there weren't any collections or deliveries due in for a while, I'd sit on some meat and read Spiderman comics.

One evening, when everyone seemed to be somewhere else and I was as usual taking advantage of the lack of supervision by sitting in the locker and reading my comics, one of the secretaries from the office upstairs came down into the warehouse. She was in her mid-thirties, tall and slim with powdery white skin. She looked like a teacher, wearing square reading glasses, always keeping her long hair up in a bun and wearing long skirts down to her sensible brown shoes. Seeing her up close, I noticed that she had a wide, smiling mouth and her blue eyes were emphasised by long black eyelashes. She hunkered down next to me in the warehouse and asked, "What you still doing down here all by yourself?"

"Reading comics," I said, not looking at her.

"Does Spiderman have a girlfriend in them comics?"

"Now, what would Spiderman want with a

girlfriend?" I asked, not sure why anyone would ask such a dumb question.

"Spiderman might want a girlfriend to do this for him," she said softly, as she slid her hand inside the top of my trousers and stuck her tongue in my ear. I was so shocked that I didn't even look up from the comic as she fondled me and bit my neck. Then she unzipped my pants and she dropped her skirt at the same time. She pulled the comic from my hand and threw it to the ground. I didn't even look at it.

She pushed me back onto the nearest slab of meat, with my pants bunched up around my ankles, and gently lowered herself on top of me, rubbing herself against me back and forth. It felt like nothing on earth and after a few minutes I felt as if my body was going to explode. I felt my eyes glaze over and I couldn't focus on anything. Then it ended. I looked up and saw her face above me in the middle of all the dead meat hanging from the ceiling, a vision that was both perfect and clear.

Needless to say, that was my first sexual experience. Every summer between the ages of eleven and eighteen, that secretary and I made love nearly every single day, dead cows serving as our bed, the warehouse of undelivered meat our love nest.

After my eighteenth birthday, I went away to university, a confident and hard-working young man. Unfortunately, I soon found that every sexual experience I encountered led to failure. I could never get sufficiently aroused, no matter what I tried.

Almost never, that is. One time, very late at night, I picked a girl up in the student union bar. She was fat and drunk, with stringy brown hair, and wore grubby tights and Doc Marten's. She was so drunk that by the time I noticed her, she was snatching people's drinks, gulping them down and then smashing the glasses on the floor. She finally tumbled to the floor and sprawled across the broken glass. She had little cuts all over her arms. I looked down at her, as people around her backed away for that first shocked moment. I felt an incredible sexual urge as I looked at her in her bloodied state. The most profound epiphany of my life dawned and I saw my opportunity. I swooped in.

"Clear the way, clear the way. I'm a qualified first-aider. I'll take care of her. Help me get her up. I've got a first aid kit in my room just down the hall."

It was that easy. I walked her to my room and removed the glass from her arms and legs with tweezers, but I didn't wipe up the blood, I just let it flow. I'd had to remove most of her clothes and it was a short step to kissing her. She didn't resist, in fact she didn't seem to mind at all. Her breath smelled of beer and kebabs, but nothing could stop me. I was so turned on by the blood trickling down her body and seeping into the sheets that it was like being back in the warehouse again. I was in ecstasy. We fucked again and again. It was perfect. By this time she was sobering up some and of course when she finally noticed all the blood, she started screaming. I calmed her down, reminded her what had happened in the student union bar. Then I forced myself to clean her up in the shower and bandage the cuts. She asked if she could sleep over, but without all that blood it just wasn't the same. I walked her back to her room and gave her a peck on the cheek. When I got back to my room, I took one look at the bloodied sheets and instantly became ragingly aroused again. That's the moment when I knew that blood played a major part in my sexuality.

The next morning I found myself down at all the local butchers, trying to find out if any of them had daughters who worked in the shop. All through my time in university, I dated one butcher's daughter after another. But none of them lasted very long because, sooner or later, every girl wants to make love somewhere besides the meat storage fridge.

You see how easy it is to end up like me. It could happen to anyone. I reckon a shrink would say that because my adolescent sexual development took place wholly amongst the bloody carcasses of animals, my sexual urges have become abnormally fixated with blood. In other words, some people like rubber, some people like leather and whips, I like blood and that was my predicament.

My life was so lonely. No one to go to see the new *Psycho* movie with, no one to go to theme restaurants with and eat very rare steak, nobody to watch cable reruns of *From Dusk till Dawn* with. All I wanted was someone who accepted me for what I was: just a normal guy with what some might consider a slightly abnormal sexual tendency.

And that's how it started. Out of sheer, mind-numbing loneliness, sometimes late at night I would jump in the car and cruise the highway looking for hitch-hiking girls who might also be lonely. But none of them understood me. They all freaked the minute the knife came out, and that's when I would mess up. I really never meant to kill them. It would escalate so quickly and once I'd started I just couldn't stop, most of the time it wouldn't even register that they'd stopped screaming, stopped moving even. Then afterwards I'd feel so bad. I'd sit in my car and just cry because it'd happened again.

For days afterwards, I'd convince myself that it would never happen again. I'd just be celibate and meditate and try to come to some inner peace, because in a world full of sexual abnormalities, it seemed that there was no room for mine. Nothing worked though, and slowly I'd feel myself drawn to the car at night, and before a month was up I was back driving around the M25 looking for hikers.

One night, as the rain beat down in heavy droplets illuminated by the oncoming headlights, I began to think, really think, about the kind of life I was leading; how it had come to this, roaming up and down the highway like some sort of sick night predator in the hopeless hope that somebody out there in the dark wet night would understand me for what I am. I was just about to turn around, head back home and curl up with the latest Anne Rice novel when I saw her drenched silhouette up ahead. I couldn't help it – I drove up, pulled over and wound down the window.

"Where are you going?" I asked.

"Wherever you're going, I guess," she said.

I almost groaned out loud. "Hop in."

She was utterly beautiful even without blood. Her damp curly hair hung down to her square shoulders. Her honey-coloured skin was flawless and wet. She wore army-issue khaki shorts over long legs which shot down to her brown Timberland boots in one smooth line. She shuffled off her backpack, tossed it into the back seat and climbed in beside me. I started driving, desperately hoping that she wouldn't end up like all the rest, knowing in my heart that she most probably would.

She looked out the windshield and the side window but never directly at me. She took off her black bomber jacket, exposing her braless chest encased in a flimsy khaki vest. We drove along the M25 in complete silence. I looked across at her at regular intervals, but she just stared out the windows. Finally, she said, "Do you like what you see?"

"Ye-ye-yes, I do" I stuttered, truly shocked for the first time since I was eleven years old.

"Then pull over." She said it like it was the most natural, and most urgent, thing in the world.

I pulled over onto the hard shoulder, the rain beating down like a chorus of applause on the roof.

She pulled my head towards her and we kissed, passionately and desperately. My hand slid down the side of my seat, feeling for that familiar cold steel, without breaking the kiss, hoping and praying all the while that she wouldn't go like all the rest. And then it happened. I thought about the inevitable ritual ahead, and I pulled away from the kiss.

"What's the matter?" she asked, breathing hard.

"Uh, nothing," I stammered, as I looked blankly at the darkness outside, my hand still damply gripping the wooden handle of the butcher's knife. She pulled me back into the kiss, one hand curved round the back of my neck.

As we kissed, my hand, still holding the butcher's knife, rose from its hiding place slowly, instinctively, but out of the corner of my nearly-closed eyes, I saw a sight I could never have imagined. It was as if I were looking in a mirror. Her hand was rising at nearly exactly the same speed, also holding a butcher's knife. We froze in one gasp, our lips were still touching, our eyes still flitting like goldfish between each other's eyes and our knives. Slowly we pulled away from the kiss, now locked in wary eye-contact, our weapons remaining raised. As if in slow-motion, we sat back in our seats and lowered our knives by our sides.

All this time I'd been looking for somebody like me, someone who would understand me. Now that I could safely assume the moment had come, I couldn't think of a thing to say. We just sat there in silence, listening to the rhythm of the rain. Suddenly, at exactly the same moment, we whipped our knives back out and faced each other. There was nothing for it but to share an embarrassed grin at how similar we were.

We slumped back in our seats and put down our knives again and started laughing, rather shyly at first but building to near hysteria. Finally, when I could catch my breath, I gasped, "Nice knife."

"Thanks," she said, still chuckling.

"Where did you get it from?"

"My father. He used to work at the local abattoir. He used to slaughter hogs."

"That's amazing! My father owned the biggest meat storage warehouse in London." My heart raced and I found myself holding both her hands in mine – not defensively, mind, but affectionately. So many new experiences in one night!

We talked for hours, sitting there in the car. I couldn't believe how many things we had in common. At last, there was someone I could talk to, someone just like me. But finally I had to ask. I paused for a while, hung my head and asked very softly if she'd ever killed anyone. She in turn hung her head and started a sniffle which grew into a full-blown blubbering cry. "Yes, I did, I killed some men, but I swear I didn't mean to, it just happened by mistake, and I tried to stop, really I did. . ."

I pulled her to my chest and hugged her and tried to console her. I said, "It's alright, it's alright, the same thing happens to me. I know you didn't mean it. When it happens to me, I don't mean it either, it just gets way out of hand. Don't worry about it. It's bound to happen to people like us who're outsiders in a world of close-minded attitudes."

With that she reached up and we started kissing, stripping off as fast as we could. As soon as we were naked, we both whipped out our knives and made tiny flesh wounds on each other's arms and stomachs. Soon the seeping blood covered most of our torsos and we pressed our bloody bodies together. The excitement made us bleed even more. It was the most perfect moment of my life. We made love in the cramped space of the car till the powder blue of dawn seeped through the windshield. She took some antiseptic lotion out of her backpack and dabbed my wounds. It stung, but in a nice way. Then it was my turn to dab her wounds. She hissed with the pain and laughed a little giggle.

We put our clothes on and I started up the car. She held my left hand, interlocking our fingers over the gearshift. The world felt like a safer place that morning as we drove down the M25 into the sun. Come to think of it, the world was a safer place that morning.

INDIAN ELVIS GIRL

My last girlfriend left me because she thought I was too competitive. She said all I thought about was making loads of money through exploitation and that I was spiritually bereft, "You've got bad karma," she said. I'll show her, I thought, as I bought the ticket to India. So I land in Goa looking for some spiritual enlightenment. I'm gonna get me some spiritual enlightenment, goddammit. I'm gonna be as wise as Deepak Chopra and Mahatma Gandhi in debate at a soothsayers, convention. I'm gonna be a big player in the wisdom stakes. Hell, I might even start a company and sell it. I'll call it, uh, I'll call it enlightenment-in-a-can and I'll copyright it. My name will be synonymous with enlightenment around the world, just like burgers and Macdonalds. She'll be sorry she ever called me unenlightened.

So I walk out the airport and the stifling heat hits me like the fiery breath of a dragon with slight halitosis. I jump into one of the cabs at the airport to try and get myself into the nearest Hilton with air conditioning, satellite TV and a complimentary bar. So I jump in the taxi, which looks like nothing more than a giant sardine can with wheels, and shout for the driver to take me to the Hilton.

As soon as we are about to pull off, I hear the door open beside me and in jumps this woman dressed like Elvis circa his Las Vegas comeback. She has on a white jumpsuit with sequins on the shoulder, and mirrored reflective shades and has a ludicrously tall quiff. She shouts something to the driver in Gujerati and he nods back to her though his rear-view mirror.

"What's going on here?" I shout.

"Oh, do not worry," she replies, in her thick Indian accent. "I am taking you to see something very beautiful."

"I don't want to see something very beautiful," I reply. "I want to go to my hotel this instant."

"We go to your hotel later, but first I must show you something of great beauty."

"Listen, driver, let me out."

"No, no," she smiles, "I'm afraid we cannot do that." As the driver ignores me completely.

We zoom past the Hilton hotel at an incredible speed and I start shouting out the window for help and she says, "Why are you bothering to shout? You are in India now, nobody will help you."

After about twenty minutes of frantic shouting I begin to lose my voice and I slump back into the cracked leather of the seat, resigned to my fate. The road spins out before us like spider's webs. As we head out of the city I can see fields of rice and green hills in the distance. The roads are now dirt tracks as the dust swirls under our churning wheels.

"How far is it to where we're going?" I ask.

"About two and a half hours."

"Two and a half hours!" I shout.

"Shh, there is something very important that I need to be telling you. I have been loving you for a very long time now."

"You've only just met me."

"Since I've met you then, and I think that it is time that we should be kissing."

As she leans toward me I turn my face away.

"Do you like Elvis?" she asks, trying to break the tension.

"No."

"How could you not like Elvis?" she asks, and launches into a tune, but she's singing all the wrong words. "You can do what you wanna do, but don't sweat on my New Age blues." I can't help but laugh, and this only encourages her. She sings song after song with the right melody but with the wrong lyrics, in a broad Indian accent. "A pink dove, we all look up."

By this time tears of laughter are rolling down my cheeks. She stops singing to ask me, if Elvis wasn't any good why did I think he was loved all over the world?

"It was probably because he used to be an ordinary trucker who got to wear lots of sparkly clothes, travel around the world and fart anytime he felt like it, without having to apologize."

"Do you think that's what people really want, to fart when and where they want?"

"Yes, probably."

"If two people were in love they could fart on each other."

"I've never been that much in love."

"You see, there are many things that you have missed: love and Elvis, that is why it's important that I show you great beauty to make up for this."

Just then we make a sharp turn off the road, driving between some coconut trees, which eventually spread apart to reveal the muscular breaking waves of the sea, as the driver cuts his engine off. He leans his head back and closes his eyes and the Indian Elvis girl leads me outside and puts down a blanket and tells me to sit and look towards the west. She sits directly behind me, playing with my hair, with one arm around my waist, as we look on the infinity of sea and sky. We watch the sun dip into the sea and look at its own reflection melting the sky into pink rippling clouds. The warm breeze of the day is coming in off the ocean and it is now as calm as a sheet of glass. Darkness falls and the stars peek out like diamonds on a black velvet sheet and we see the reflection of each star rippling on the sea. The waves lisp quietly against the white crescent shore and the moon comes out as if someone has cut a circle from the cloth sky. Such boundless beauty leaves me hypnotized.

The Indian Elvis girl asks me if I like it and I tell her it's the most beautiful thing I have ever seen.

"Good, I'll take you back to your hotel now."

In the car I reach into my bag to offer her some money. "You westerners don't understand, do you? I

114

don't want your money. You can't buy beautiful things or beautiful experiences. There is no amount of money that can pay for what we enjoyed today. I just wanted to share something beautiful with you that's all. That's all." As she begins to sob. We sit in silence all the way, watching the oncoming lights of the city in the distance.

MILLENNIUM

My girlfriend broke up with me on Christmas Day 1999. She said she was starting the millennium with a new phase of her life that didn't include me. So my New Year's night was set to be the most miserable one in history. I did the thing any typical man would do: I rang around all my ex-girlfriends to see if any of them were free. None of them were available. How could I expect them to be? I mean, nobody would be free for the biggest party of our lifetime. I heard that people had booked reservations in restaurants up to a year before. Everybody knew who he or she would be with on that night at least six months ago. Even if they didn't know, they had at least six months to work on it. It was typical of my girlfriend to break up with me a week before New Year. I thought I would definitely end up alone with a TV dinner, and a whopping depression.

It was then that I got a call from my cousin, saying that he'd heard that I was now single and that I could come out with him, his girlfriend, and his girlfriend's cousin on a sort of millennium blind date. Now, past experiences with my cousin when he's tried to set me up have been disastrous. There's one thing worse than spending the New Year alone, and that is to spend it with someone ugly and uninteresting. So I said no, no way! My cousin then set about with the most convincing of arguments as to why I should come. He said that she was more attractive than his girlfriend, and the reason that she was single was that she was nineteen and her parents were very strict. She was staying over at his girlfriend's house and she couldn't leave her home. The clincher was that he'd pay for the whole night. He already had reservations for four at a four-star restaurant and at one of the most exclusive parties at the Hilton hotel. He said even if I were to find a better option I wouldn't be able to get in anywhere because he knew that I just wasn't organised enough to get it together. So I said OK, but with one stipulation: that I get to see what she looks like before the night. He said that it would be no problem because he'd be picking them up from an aerobics class later that night, so he'd swing by.

Waiting in the car outside the aerobics class, my cousin yapped on about how great this girl was. I ignored him and looked through the window. As I looked past the glare of the car park lights, I saw the distant shape of two women coming towards the car. I stopped staring through the window and just waited for them. They opened their doors simultaneously; my cousin's girlfriend sat in front while her cousin sat in the back with me.

One look at her and I was transfixed. She was dreamily beautiful. My cousin had not lied. She had the body of a top-class athlete – all taut and tight. Her skin was flawless. She had a long elegant neck. Her jet-black hair flowed like Indian ink to the centre of her back. She had piercing hazel eyes with light streaks and her lips were wide and full. She smelled clean and fresh, somewhere between Palmolive soap and lemon. I couldn't believe my luck.

My cousin turned around and said "Robert this is Anna. Anna this is Robert."

Without a word she put out her hand to shake mine and pulled me forward and gave me a tiny peck on my lips. I was somewhat taken aback, not being used to being greeted this way by somebody that I'd just met, but then she smiled, all tight eyed with a perfect row of teeth, and I smiled back. In that moment I felt like I'd known her for years. She held my hand and did not let it go. My cousin started the car and as we drove and she stared mysteriously out the open window, her hair being slightly tossed by the breeze. She was still holding onto my hand, gently passing her fingers over the peaks of my knuckles. I tried not to stare, but I couldn't help it.

We got to their house and she leaned in to hold me behind my neck, and kissed me on my eyelids, raised her shoulders and flashed another one of her beautiful smiles and backed out of the car door. My cousin kissed his girlfriend goodbye and we drove away.

He asked excitedly, "Well? What d' you think?"

"What do I think? I think she's fantastic!"

119

"So it's on for New Year's, right?"

"Hell yes!"

That New Year's night I couldn't decide what to wear. I had bought a new suit, but on the night I thought the other suits I had were a better fit, so I wore an old one. I stepped into the car and we made our way to pick up the girls. Parked outside their house I felt my stomach flutter as they walked towards the car. She stepped delicately into the back seat in her ankle length dress. She looked even more beautiful than when I had seen her the last time. She immediately took hold of my hand, taking up where she had left off from last time we met. I thought to myself that this was going to be the best New Year's night ever.

My cousin drove to an off-licence and he and his girlfriend got out of the car to choose some champagne.

I turned to Anna and said, "You look beautiful. I'm very proud to be starting the millennium with you."

She looked back at me and smiled and said, "Grrrrruuuuaaaah," in a tone slightly reminiscent of Chewbacca in *Star Wars*. I stared, confused by her response, and then she did it again, "Grrruuuuuuaaah," and then she pulled out a little notepad and pen and scribbled hurriedly. "I'm proud 2 B here with U 2."

That's when it dawned on me that she was deaf. Just then my cousin and his girlfriend came back to the car and I asked him to come with me for a minute because there were a few things I wanted to get. Inside the off-licence I said to him angrily, "What the hell is wrong with you? Why didn't you tell me she was deaf?"

"Don't worry, she can read lips."

"That is not the point and you know it!"

"I know, I know, I'm sorry. If I'd told you that she was deaf from the outset you wouldn't even have met her. You said yourself how great she was when you met her. You can't pull out now – you'll just fuck everything up. Come on, it's millennium New Year. So what if she's deaf?"

"Let me ask you something. Would you be with a deaf woman?"

"If she was as lovely as Anna, of course I would."

"How are we supposed to communicate, for God's sake? God, I knew this was too good to be true."

"How have you been communicating this far? Look, she's deaf but she's not stupid. You make it sound like she's a retard. She can understand you when you speak, and she can communicate but it's a different, that's all. Come on, let's just have a good time."

So I thought that I should just be polite, and enjoy the night and just leave it at that. We went back to the car and we were on our way. Anna kept looking across at me in the car. It was obvious to her that my mood had changed. I could feel her staring at me as I stared out the window. She moved over to my side of the seat and took my hand placed it on the centre of her chest, and looked up at me, with those hypnotic eyes, taking on a look of deep melancholy. Without any words I knew exactly what she meant. She looked into my eyes then looked at my lips, then looked into my eyes and then looked at my lips and then looked into my eyes and looked at my lips again, and I leaned forward to kiss her. As we kissed she nibbled on my bottom lip and passed her tongue around my gums. I had never kissed like that before.

After that I understood what my cousin was talking about. She communicated affection, not through subtle conversation but through intimacy and the realms of sensation. We had a great New Year's night and of the new millennium found me buying a book on sign language, to see if I could learn a language she could understand.

ACKNOWLEDGEMENTS

I am grateful for the encouragement I have received in the writing of Adventures in 3D. There are far too many friends and artists who have helped, inspired and encouraged for me to mention them all here. You know who you are. Finally, this book would not have come into being with out the specific help of Bernadine Evaristo and Ruth Borthwick in their time at Spread The Word, Geraldine Collinge at Apples and Snakes. My agent, Melanie Abrahams at Renaissance One and Colin Channer, Kwame Dawes Ninety, Nia Roberts, Miranda Baker, Maja Prausnitz and the London Arts Board.

Women I've Known and Meals I've Cooked
by Charlie Dark

A collection of poetry, prose and easy recipes for the single male, from the mind of the retired B-Boy Charlie Dark. The long-awaited debut from the man behind the Urban Poets Society and the beat sonics of Attica Blues. He returns to his writing roots to feed the hungry.

The Essential Booker
by Malika Booker

One of the UK's premier performers, Malika Bookers has earned increasing fame for her touching monologues, poems and stories. *The Essential Booker* brings together the best of ten years of work, providing the most comprehensive view of her mecurial talent.

So You Want to Make the Sherpa Smile?
by Samantha Coerbell

A collection of poems and stories from Samantha Coerbell, already reknowned for being the opening act for Me'shell Ndege Ocello, and touring with Nuyorican Poets Live. Samantha Coerbell returns with her moving street-smart tales.